"I don't have any room in my life for a woman."

Jon Alexander stopped, watching Holly rise from the sofa, a fleeting smile on his lips. "An affair's one thing. But you're the sort of woman a man falls in love with."

Was he implying that he was falling in love with her? Eyes shining, Holly opened her mouth to speak.

Jon cut her off. "Love and marriage are complications that would get in the way of my research," he said sharply, seeming to read her thoughts. "And it's my work that's important to me, not my personal life."

Your work's important to me, too, and I could help you with it, Holly wanted to scream at him. *Then you could have me and your work.* Her heart plummeted. She had only a handful of weeks to prove it to him. But there had to be a way.

Emily Spenser admits she was envious when her husband sold his first mystery novel. So in 1982 she sat down and wrote *Chateau Villon* for Harlequin Romance and has been writing ever since. Now she and her husband share interesting careers that combine travel with creative work. They live in Sequim, Washington, and when they're not writing or taking trips to research backgrounds for future books, they can be found exploring the mountains and coastlines, clamming or trying to learn the game of golf.

Books by Emily Spenser

These books may be available at your local bookseller.

Don't miss any of our special offers. Write to us at the following address for information on our newest releases.

Harlequin Reader Service
901 Fuhrmann Blvd., P.O. Box 1397, Buffalo, NY 14240
Canadian address: P.O. Box 603,
Fort Erie, Ont. L2A 5X3

Unlikely Lovers
Emily Spenser

Harlequin Books

TORONTO • NEW YORK • LONDON
AMSTERDAM • PARIS • SYDNEY • HAMBURG
STOCKHOLM • ATHENS • TOKYO • MILAN

Original hardcover edition published in 1986
by Mills & Boon Limited

ISBN 0-373-02813-X

Harlequin Romance first edition January 1987

CHAPTER ONE

As Holly deftly removed the cork from the bottle of burgundy, her ears caught the faint whine of an aeroplane's engine. With the sound her heart suddenly raced. Only one guest was scheduled to arrive at the inn by chartered plane that evening, and that was Dr Jon Alexander. It had to be him! Her cornflower-blue eyes sparkled with excitement. This time tomorrow, incredible as it seemed, she'd be out in the rain forest ... actually collecting botanical specimens with him! It was the dream of a lifetime.

With reluctance Holly brought her mind back to a more immediate reality. 'I think you'll find this dry enough,' she said, concentrating with some difficulty as she poured half an inch of wine into the glass.

The balding, middle-aged man swirled the dark liquid, sniffed it with his eyes rapturously closed, and then took a small sip. 'Delightful,' he said after a moment. 'Bold, but not overly aggressive. A trifle precocious, but not insolently so.'

She bit back a smile. It was quite a tribute to the house wine at three dollars fifty a bottle, but his female companion seemed duly impressed. Holly poured a glass for her, then filled the man's and set the bottle down on the table.

With all of her customers attended to for the

moment, she headed to the distant empty section
of the restaurant to peer through the big windows
at Lake Quinault, its muted blue sparkling in the
remnants of patchy evening sunlight. Pretending to
straighten an already perfect setting on the corner
table, Holly watched as the little, blue-and-
white Cessna 210, fitted with pontoons, landed
smoothly on the placid lake. It slowed, turned, and
taxied towards the Quinault Valley Inn's wooden
dock.

Only one person emerged from the plane: a tall,
broad-shouldered man who jumped down from
the Cessna's doorway on to the dock with athletic
ease. Holly waited for someone else to follow him;
certainly *this* wasn't the world-renowned botanist.
He was too young, too ... too ...

While she watched, Anne, a fellow part-time
waitress, appeared at her side. They saw the tall
man swing a suitbag over his shoulder, then with
his free hand take the large, loaded backpack the
pilot pushed off the plane to him. He walked off
the dock and up the pathway across the sloping
lawn, carrying the pack easily in one hand, as if it
weighed five pounds not fifty. The path, which led
to the lobby entrance, skirted the dining-room so
they got a good look at him as he walked by.

'*That*'s Dr Alexander?' Anne whispered, her
elfin face suddenly filled with envy. 'You've been
holding out on me, Holly Fraser!' she complained
ruefully. 'I had no idea your idol was so attractive
or I would have paid more attention when you
raved about him.'

'I didn't rave, and he's not my idol,' Holly

whispered back warmly. To be honest, of course, he was, but Anne, who was her roommate at college and who was rarely serious about anything, would tease her unmercifully if she admitted it. 'As you very well know,' Holly added, looking askance at her friend, 'it's just that he's one of America's most eminent botanists, and I admire and respect his work. And that's all.'

Actually Holly was more than a bit overawed by Alexander's looks. If she'd thought about his appearance—which she hadn't, being more interested in the scientist than the man—she might have hazarded a guess that he'd be meek-looking and retiring, with thick horn-rimmed glasses, rounded shoulders, and a shallow chest—the results of long hours hunched over a microscope.

Whatever she had imagined, it wasn't this virile-looking six feet two or so of lean male in his early thirties, with thick, deep russet-coloured hair, who, moreover, was dressed in an expensive and well-tailored Shetland wool sports jacket with suede elbow patches, a pale green shirt and brown slacks. The man radiated an overwhelming aura of sophistication—casual, confident sophistication—and wealth. She might have guessed about the wealth, if she'd given it any thought. Anyone who established and supported his own private research institute had to have money. Lots of it.

'Well, if *that*'s all,' Anne drawled, as they watched the object of their fervent attention disappear into the lobby doorway, 'then I'll seat him in my section if he comes in for dinner. Yum!' Holly hadn't fooled her for a moment. 'I feel a severe case of hero worship of my own coming on.'

'You wouldn't!'

Anne looked solemn. 'Why not? After all, you get to go on a field trip with the man for three whole days!' Then unable to keep a straight face any longer, because her friend, usually so calm and collected, looked positively flustered, she broke into a broad smile. 'I'm just teasing, Holly. He's all yours. But I hope you're at least going to introduce me if you get the chance. He's bound to have some absolutely divine friends.'

'Anne, really,' Holly whispered in not-quite-convincing indignation. 'The only thing about Dr Jon Alexander that interests me in the least is his brain!'

As Jon Alexander strode through the old-fashioned lobby with its massive stone fireplace and comfortable wicker furniture, he toyed with the idea of skipping a hot dinner and having a sandwich and a Scotch sent up to his room instead.

He smiled wryly to himself. Lillian, his matronly lab technician, was right. He *was* turning into a recluse. A natural mother hen, she had recently been clucking about just that. That and more.

'Furthermore,' she had said, 'you're working yourself to death. You need a break—a change of scene, even if it's just for a couple of days.'

'Look, Lillian, I've just made a breakthrough in my research,' he answered, trying to rub the tension out of his temples and wishing she'd leave him alone so he could get on with his work. 'I need to follow it up. By the way, have you phoned round yet to find me a local mycologist who's familiar with the Olympic rain forest? I need that assortment of fresh plant material as soon as possible.'

'Of course I did, but I could only find a kid,' Lillian said, her tone doubtful, 'a student from Port Angeles College, who was raised at Lake Quinault and is supposed to be quite knowledge-able—and who has a brother who's a park ranger there. The brother—Clint Fraser, I think his name is—really came in handy. He's already taken care of the permit you have to have to pick anything in the rain forest, and he's even offered to go along on the field trip. All the same, I think you ought to consider going too—to supervise, I mean.' She paused, then craftily added, 'Of course, that means you'd have to spend three days tramping down forest trails and camping out under the stars.'

Jon, seeing right through her, scowled, yet Lillian had succeeded in conjuring up a sudden, beguiling picture of cool, misty air, verdant vegetation, and a crystal-clear mountain lake. The images floated seductively through his mind, contrasting sharply with the sterile white walls and neon lights of the lab. It had been months since he'd done any of his own field work, and he missed it. Certainly now that his research was taking him into mycology, an area of botany he knew relatively little about as yet, he really could stand to get some first-hand collecting experience. And, of course, there was the lure of that clean, cool, unpopulated forest.

The friendly welcome of the Quinault Valley

Inn's receptionist brought Jon back to the present.

'I've given you a third-floor room, very quiet, with a view of the lake,' said the young man with modish wire-rimmed glasses, as he handed Jon a key. 'The dining-room's open until nine, and you won't need a reservation. Our summer season's over now, no more crowds.'

The information did not surprise him. His flight from the Institute, located near Sequim, a small town on the north side of Washington State's remote and mountainous Olympic Peninsula, had taken a little over an hour, and from the air he'd seen dozens of loaded logging trucks on Highway 101, but few passenger cars and campers. And once the little aeroplane had cleared the northwest flank of the Olympic mountains and turned south down the coast there were almost none.

He couldn't blame the fair-weather tourists for decamping from the west side—or the Wet Side, as the natives called it. During the rainy season that loomed ahead, the ocean-facing, western valleys of the peninsula—the Hoh, Queets, and the one he was in, the Quinault—would get almost a hundred and fifty inches of rain, a superabundance of moisture that clothed these valleys with the only rain forest in the northern hemisphere. It also chased away all but the most hardy and adventurous visitors, the water-resistant locals—mostly lumberjacks, fishermen, and national park personnel—and the Indians whose ancestors had already been there for four thousand years when the first European rowed ashore in 1775 to claim the land for King Carlos of Spain.

Wet as it was, Jon reflected with satisfaction that the climate was ideal for at least one thing: mycology, the study of that teeming family of primitive plants lacking chlorophyll such as mushrooms, which had drawn him here and had injected such an exciting new note into his research.

The climate was good for something else, too, he mused a while later when he walked into the dining-room: protecting a delicate complexion from the roughening effect of too much sun.

Standing at the entrance, waiting to be seated, his eyes had fallen—and stayed—on a tall, slender young woman caught in the last warm, golden glow of the evening sun that reflected from Lake Quinault and poured through a large window. He stood rooted, his mind suddenly far away from mushrooms and chlorophyll. Some carping connoisseur might find fault with her, he supposed: her nose was a shade too short, her mouth a trifle too generous to label her a classic beauty. Still, with her complexion of pure ivory tinted with the barest hint of transparent pink on her high cheekbones, her sensual red lips, and her long, glossy black hair, she was like a wild English rose that had been magically transplanted to this remote corner of the world. She turned her head, lifted eyes bordered with long, luxuriant lashes, and seemed to catch sight of him. Exquisite, cornflower-blue eyes as clear and clean as the lake itself fixed on him and held him rooted.

The name tag, the simple peasant-style tan

blouse, and the brown wrapover skirt (what drab, lacklustre colours for her!) marked her as one of the waitresses. So did her hair style: all that lovely, thick hair was pulled severely back and held by a clip at the nape of her neck. The sudden, strong desire to walk up to her and free her hair so that he could see what it looked like spilling over her shoulders and framing that face brought him up short. Jon frowned slightly. He had no wish to become involved with anyone. He didn't have the time for it. And he was past the age when quick one-night stands held any attraction for him. Not that this young woman looked like the type who would jump into bed with a man at the first come-on—despite the disturbing, intoxicating fact that her eyes were still riveted on his.

There was an air of youthful innocence about her, although obviously she had to be old enough to work in a restaurant that served alcohol. No doubt it was merely the refreshing and unusual absence of heavy make-up on her face that made her seem so fresh and dewy, he thought cynically, a frown creasing his forehead. Innocence was quite out of fashion these days, even here, he imagined, on the Olympic Peninsula.

His deepening frown made the young woman realise she was staring. With a wash of delicate colour flooding her cheeks, she turned abruptly away, hurriedly reached for a nearby coffee pot, and then was off refilling the coffee cups of the few remaining diners. So much for any fantasies he'd been starting to hatch. Not that he'd hatched any. He was here for saprophytes and perthophytes, not for—well, never mind.

His frown must have intensified even more, because a second waitress, hurrying towards him, menu in hand, approached him as if she expected to be bitten.

'I'm sorry to keep you waiting so long, sir,' she stammered apologetically, although he couldn't have been standing there more than a minute. 'This way please,' she said, her hazel eyes bright with trepidation.

Following her to a table near the window, Jon was relieved that this unperturbing young woman would be his waitress. Actually, with her gamine look, her sprinkling of freckles, and her soft brown curls framing a pretty face, she too was attractive enough, but after the other one she was like a common-variety daisy.

Daisies ... roses ... cornflowers ... what the hell was the matter with him? Being a botanist was no excuse for these repulsive flights of hackneyed drivel. Opening his menu, Jon sat there glowering at it. Perhaps he was just hungry, More than one girlfriend had told him he became grouchy as a bear when he was.

'Would you care for a cocktail this evening?'

The voice was soft and vibrant, sensuous and guileless at the same time. He knew who it belonged to before he looked up. Was he in *her* section after all? What had happened to the freckle-faced waitress?

The lines of his mouth thinned with irrational anger as he looked up to find those luscious blue eyes gazing at him, quite serene and composed, but touched with a little—what? Was it awe? Not likely. It was probably shock. No doubt this was the first time in her experience that a male customer had scowled at the sight of her.

'Scotch on the rocks,' he said abruptly, his nerves and muscles stretched taut. God, did he need a drink. 'A tall one.'

She caught her bottom lip for an instant with her teeth, as if she'd been on the verge of saying something, but had found herself deserted by her courage. After an awkward pause, all she said finally was, 'I'll bring it right away,' and fled.

A recluse, and now an ogre who goes around scaring nice young women. With a shake of his head over what he hoped was out-of-character behaviour, Jon pulled a small, black notebook out of his jacket pocket. He was never without one. His mind had the irritating habit of producing fresh approaches to research problems when he was thinking—or thought he was thinking—of some totally unrelated subject. Tonight he couldn't fool himself into pretending that any creative ideas were about to burst forth, but by jotting down some possible experimental models he could use once he got back to the laboratory, he could at least get his mind back on important things like work.

The strategy was so successful that by the time the waitress returned with his drink, he'd recovered enough of his equilibrium to give her a perfunctory, mechanical smile.

'Have you decided what you'd like to order yet?' she asked, setting down the drink.

'What kind of salmon do you serve?' Jon

inquired, hazarding a guess that, as in all good northwest coast restaurants, this regional delicacy would be on the menu. Odd—he remembered staring at the menu when he'd first sat down, but he couldn't recall anything on it. And Dr Jon Alexander was famous for his ability to concentrate. No, this was not his night.

'Blueback,' she answered. Her voice was husky with nervousness.

Jon's eyes flicked to her name tag, and he suppressed a smile. Holly, it said in big, black letters. Roses, daisies, cornflowers ... and now holly. Holly—*Ilex aquifolium*—a perfect botanical name for her. And how magnificent red would look on her, the exact shade of the crimson berries on the glossy, evergreen shrub she was named after. She shifted uneasily while he stared at her nameplate. Probably she thought she had a nut on her hands.

'It's caught in the lake by the Quinault Indians, and it's quite delicious,' she said tentatively. 'If you've never tried it, I'd recommend it.'

'It sounds fine.' He would have said sawdust sounded fine just to get rid of her provocative, unsettling presence. 'And I'll have a half-bottle of Chablis to go with it.'

He tore his green eyes from the retreating form that moved with unconscious grace towards the door to the kitchen and buried himself in his notebook, or tried to.

When she returned with the wine and a pewter ice bucket, he acknowledged her with no more than a brief nod, and kept busy with the notebook. The nonsense he was now scribbling could be torn out easily enough later on.

Holly removed the foil strip from the mouth of the bottle and twisted in the corkscrew. Out of the corner of his eye, Jon could see that her gaze kept drifting in his direction instead of focusing on her task. Thus, when she pulled up on the corkscrew, he wasn't surprised when the cork didn't come out with a satisfying pop. In fact, she'd spilt it, and most of the cork hadn't come out at all. It had been a mistake to order a bottle. Few people are good at opening them, and all he'd really wanted was a glass anyway.

'Oh, dear . . .'

Jon stopped writing and regarded her with one eyebrow raised. She looked so dismayed that the hard line of his mouth softened.

'Looks like you're having trouble.'

'A little,' she replied, but there was a stubborn little tilt to her chin that clearly said she wouldn't appreciate an offer of help. 'I think I can get it out.'

'Opening a wine bottle can be tricky,' he said sympathetically, thawing a little further. She was independent; he liked that.

Trying to twist the corkscrew back into the crumbling cork, she smiled gratefully at him. That was a mistake. Distracted, she'd exerted too much force and had pushed the cork all the way in.

'Now I've done it,' she exclaimed ruefully, then added quickly, 'I'll go and get another bottle.'

She'd made the offer with composure, yet she would no doubt have to pay for a second bottle out of her tips, Jon reflected, tips that would be scanty on a Sunday evening in late September with only a handful of guests.

He waved a dismissive hand. 'Don't worry about it. What's a little cork? The wine will pour easily enough once you get it started.'

But getting it started wasn't easy and Jon could see she was rattled by the time she left the table. By now she was probably as anxious to be done with him as he was with her.

Sipping his wine, he stared reflectively out of the window. As soon as he had made a start on this new phase in his work, he would take a couple of weeks off after all and fly back east for a vacation. It was more apparent than ever how much he needed one, and uncomfortably obvious that he was in dire need of some female companionship.

Monica would fill the bill nicely. Monica, with her silvery blonde hair and that beautiful, cool elegance that made you think—at first—that she herself was cool and passionless. Monica, too restless to settle long with any man and too rich to need to had phoned not long ago to tell him she was back in circulation. Yes, he'd return her call and arrange a get-together. They could do the theatres, the clubs, all the old haunts . . .

The young woman in the drab waitress's costume, who had unknowingly caused these unexpected reflections, reappeared at his table. Jon was aware of her faint, fresh fragrance as she reached out to move the crystal water-glass slightly to make room for a miniature breadboard on which sat a small, brown wheatmeal loaf and a dish of butter squares. Setting the board down next to his opened notebook she accidently hit his full wineglass, toppling it over and snapping the stem. Jon snatched the notebook out of the path of the spreading liquid just in time.

'Damn!'

As soon as he'd said it he was sorry. He hadn't meant to swear at her. And it was partly his fault: his notebook hadn't left her much room. Not that that totally explained why a woman who moved so gracefully was so unrelievedly clumsy when it came to serving him.

'Sorry,' he said with a smile, as she frantically mopped up the wine. 'No harm done. First day on the job?'

Pink stained her cheeks as she finished cleaning up the spill and then picked up the pieces of glass. 'No ... and, honestly I'm not usually this awkward. I'll bring you a new glass and some more wine.'

'A new glass will do. There's plenty of wine still in the bottle and I hadn't planned on drinking it all. I need to make an early start of it tomorrow.'

'I—er—know ...' Holly stopped for a second, biting her lower lip in anxiety. This didn't seem like the best of times to tell him she was his trusty, competent guide. Approaching the subject indirectly, she said, 'It's just that it's exciting to see you in person, Dr Alexander. I've read your book, and all of your articles, and I admire your work so ...'

Amazed at her knowing who he was—pictures of authors rarely appear on the backs of scholarly book jackets or in journals, and he'd never allowed public tours of his Institute—Jon regarded her quizzically.

'I'm flattered. Not many people spend their spare time curled up with articles on botany. Certainly you're the first waitress I've met who has.'

'Oh, I'm only a waitress at weekends,' Holly explained, adoration leaping into her eyes. 'I'm a botany student at Port Angeles College. So is Anne—the other waitress. Your work on increased food crop productivity is the most significant research anybody has done in botany in ten years.' The words were pouring out, tumbling over one another. 'You're a tremendous inspiration to me ... I mean *us* ...'

Jon's blood froze; he remembered the last time he'd had an extended conversation with a young student with hero worship in her eyes. It had precipitated his move to this backwater of the American continent. But this time he'd damn well nip any potential problem in the bud.

'That's nice,' he said stiffly. 'I wish both of you luck with your studies.' His green eyes had turned as cold as the glacier-fed streams in the mountains behind Lake Quinault. With his mouth clamped in a rigidly straight line, he glanced openly at his watch. 'Shouldn't my dinner be ready by now?'

'I'll go and check,' Holly replied calmly, but Jon could see the hurt and confusion in those beautiful, expressive eyes.

He had meant his words to be like a slap in the face, and as rotten as it made him feel, he couldn't have helped himself. When you nipped things in the bud, as any botanist knew, it was no time to be gentle.

The sight of the food with which she quickly returned did nothing to awaken his dead appetite, but with the bewilderment and pain he'd already put in her eyes, he couldn't very well ask her to take it away and demand his bill. Sure, he'd been damaged in the past, but it certainly wasn't her fault.

'It looks delicious,' he forced himself to say. He could see that his voice wasn't convincing and he had to restrain himself from an astonishing, totally unexpected desire to gather her into his arms and kiss the hurt away.

Taken aback, he dropped his eyes to lessen the temptation, and they fell on her hands. She was reaching for the plate with steady fingers, but he could see that her grip on the serving tray wasn't firm. Before he could reach out to help, the tray tilted, sending the plate sliding towards him. It wasn't . . . it couldn't . . .

It could. It did.

Glumly, he watched the plate tip over the edge of the tray, flip, hang suspended for a brief, agonizing instant, then fall . . .

CHAPTER TWO

'RIGHT into his lap?' Clint threw his head back and guffawed.

'You're kidding!' her sister-in-law, Mary, whispered, her fingers at her lips. 'Aren't you?'

'I wish I was,' Holly said gloomily, pouring some milk into her coffee and stirring it with a spoon.

Her brother and his wife just sat there laughing. They were as bad as Anne.

'It's not funny, you two,' Holly wailed. Then remembering the look on Jon Alexander's face as the fish dinner landed in his lap, a slow grin lit her features.

'Was he angry?' Clint asked when he got his breath. 'What did he say?'

Holly looked askance at her brother to see if he was joking. He wasn't.

'A few choice words that I'll refrain from repeating, but it was something to the effect I was a walking hazard and that the government should make me wear a warning label.' She smiled ruefully. 'Seriously, though,' she said, her voice turning mournful, 'when he finds out this morning that I'm the guide he requested for this field trip, he's going to have a fit.'

'Oh, he's probably laughed it off by now,' Mary said soothingly. 'You did think to offer to pay his dry-cleaning bill, didn't you?'

'Of course,' Holly answered gloomily, 'but he didn't take me up on it. Obviously, he just didn't want anything more to do with me.' She paused, looking gravely at the hand-made ceramic coffee cup with which she was toying. 'It's not just the field trip, you know. Sure, I'll be disappointed if he doesn't want me to go with him, but it's the summer internship at his Institute in Sequim that I'm worried about.'

She shook her head. 'I was really hoping to land it. What a chance it would have been to get some first-hand experience with serious research before going on to graduate school.' Holly's expression grew bleaker and her blue eyes clouded. 'Not only that, but the stipend for the internship is really generous, remember? It would go a long way towards paying next year's expenses.'

'Oh dear.' Mary's oval face sobered as she tucked behind her ears the curtains of chin-length, straight blonde hair that had fallen forward. 'I'd forgotten about all that.'

Clint turned serious as well, and he rubbed his red-bearded jaw thoughtfully. 'So had I. But surely Jon Alexander wouldn't let a little thing like this affect the internship, would he? You'll be top in your class; you're bound to be the most qualified graduate applying.'

'He wouldn't, huh?' Holly nervously ran a finger around the rim of her cup and glanced up at her brother. 'He will if he thinks I'm plain clumsy. He'll be afraid I'll break every piece of equipment and ruin every experiment I put my hands on.'

'Hmm.' Clint frowned, his massive brow

wrinkling. 'That could be a problem. He thought for a moment. 'Well, you'll just have to show what you can do on this field trip, sis, so he can see you're not like that.' His expression brightened. 'Besides, he *needs* you, and you're exactly who he requested: the most knowledgeable mycologist on the whole peninsula. Don't worry, he'll see how competent you really are. He'll forget all about last night.'

It was true, Holly reflected, that mycology was a new interest of Jon Alexander's, and with at least fifty thousand varieties of mushrooms and related species, and four thousand of them in the rain forest alone, no one became an expert overnight, even a scientist as brilliant as he was. And she wasn't concerned about her ability to locate hundreds of species quickly for him; she knew the best collecting areas as well as the back of her hand. But would he let her have the chance to prove it?

'Maybe he'd forget about last night if the field trip went well,' Holly agreed with a little shrug, 'but I'm afraid he's not going to let me go. The minute he sees me he's going to explode.'

But there was more to it than her un-characteristic clumsiness of the night before—something she hadn't mentioned to Clint or Mary because she didn't understand it herself. From the second Jon Alexander had walked through the door of the restaurant and their eyes had met, a jolting shock of physical awareness had sprung up between them. Her own reaction Holly attributed to hero worship. But what about his reaction to her? It certainly couldn't have been any deep attraction—the opposite would have been closer to the truth, considering the way he never stopped scowling at her. And when she had told him she was a botany student and that he was an inspiration to her, he'd glared at her as if she'd turned into the creature from the Black Lagoon right before his eyes. You'd have thought he'd be flattered, not infuriated or whatever he was. It was no wonder she got so rattled that she dropped his dinner. In fact, it served him right!

Clint, reaching over with a big hand and tugging playfully at her thick braid of hair, broke into her thoughts.

'You just finish your breakfast, Holly, and stop worrying. I'll smooth things out with Jon Alexander.'

He would, too, if anybody could. Holly gave her big brother a grateful smile. He'd always been there for her, and even if he was over-protective at times, she owed him more than she could ever repay. Eight years older than she, he'd just finished college when the Saturday salmon-fishing party their parents had gone on turned into a double tragedy. The powerful rogue wind whipping down the straits had hit the small sailboat broadside, catching it on the crest of a wave, and flipping it over like a bath toy; their parents who had been below in the galley were the only casualties.

Although a distant aunt and uncle in the midwest had come forward to offer the fourteen-year-old Holly a home, Clint wouldn't even entertain the thought of them being separated. Luckily, he was offered a job as a park ranger in Olympic National Park, and with it had come a house in the ranger compound at Lake Quinault. So he had been able to provide Holly with a home without uprooting her or himself from the remote area in which they'd been born and which they loved so much.

Now, Holly spent most of the week living in a college dormitory some hundred and fifteen miles away in Port Angeles, returning here only at weekends to work at the nearby lodge. But this house was still home, and Clint and Mary (whom Clint had married a year ago to Holly's genuine delight) were the only family she had.

'Hey, both of you better hurry and finish eating,' Mary admonished affectionately, passing Clint the muffin basket, 'or you'll be late. It's almost seven and Mike's going to be here to pick you up in just a few minutes.'

Clint took another wild blueberry muffin with alacrity before handling the basket to Holly. 'Are you sure you don't want to go with us, honey?' he asked, turning back to his wife. 'There's still time for you to change your mind.'

'Why don't you, Mary?' Holly interjected, spreading a muffin with butter. Although her sister-in-law was definitely the domestic type, Mary was lots of fun on the outings she was talked into going on—not to mention the fact that she could cook rings around both Holly and her brother. The heavenly, light-as-air muffin Holly was biting into was a prime example, but she could perform almost equal wonders with camp food. 'Three whole days of relaxing and sleeping under the stars. Doesn't that sound lovely?'

'Three days of slogging in the rain and going without hot showers, you mean!' Mary scoffed, shaking her blonde head. 'No, thanks. I'm planning on sewing myself a new outfit and reading a couple of good books in front of a cosy fire, while you two are off collecting smelly, mouldy, old . . . funguses! Ugh!'

Holly caught Clint's eye and they both laughed. Mary's squeamishness about the decayed vegetable matter Holly sometimes dragged home was a standing joke.

They heard Mike's four-wheel-drive Jeep estate pulling to a stop in front of the house as they were clearing the breakfast dishes. While Clint said goodbye to Mary, Holly went out to start loading the equipment and supplies. Ferny and Dipper, Mike's two packhorses, now comfortably installed in a horse trailer behind the estate car, would transport the bulk of the material, but each person would be responsible for carrying his or her personal gear in a backpack: rain ponchos, tube tents, sleeping bags, and extra clothes.

Mike jumped out to help. Sandy-haired with a ready smile, he was a shade over six feet, like her brother, but where Clint was husky, with muscles developed from early summer jobs as a lumberjack, his friend was lanky and long-limbed.

'We left you a cup of coffee,' Holly said, 'in case you wanted one before we got on the road. And some blueberry muffins, unless Clint has demolished them all.'

'No, thanks.' Mike stowed away the gear as Holly handed it to him. 'I had breakfast before I left. Did you have any trouble getting the time off from college?'

Holly shook her head. 'Not when I explained why I wanted it. My professors were more than willing to let me go. They thought it would be a great opportunity for me.' Little did they know, she thought with grim humour as she handed Mike the box of groceries, that it had so far proved an opportunity for disaster.

'Did you get a chance to meet Jon Alexander yesterday?' Mike asked as he secured the load with a tarpaulin.

'You might say that,' Holly answered ruefully, deciding she'd better recount last night's débâcle to Mike. There might be quite a scene ahead of them at the inn when they picked Alexander up.

Predictably, Mike was laughing by the time she'd finished.

'And you're telling me he doesn't know you're his guide?' he chortled.

'I'm afraid not,' Holly confessed sheepishly. 'To put it mildly, an appropriate moment never seemed to present itself. I was too busy breaking, spilling or dropping something.'

Mike gave a low whistle, then exclaimed, 'Man, I can't wait to see this guy's face when he finds out.'

He didn't have long to wait. Jon Alexander, dressed like the rest of them in a jacket, jeans, woollen shirt and hiking boots, and carrying his backpack, was coming out of the inn's main entrance when Clint, Holly, and Mike drove up the curved driveway. An unmistakable look of dismay rippled over the scientist's features as he saw Holly climb out with her brother.

Regarding him with as steady a gaze as she could manage, considering that her heart had begun to race at the sight of him, Holly watched his dismay change swiftly to grim determination. It didn't take any clairvoyance on her part to know exactly what he was so grimly determined about. Undoubtedly he assumed that one of the two men was his guide, and that she was going to ask if she could tag along. A highly definitive No was chiselled on his face.

Well, if there was anything she could do about it, he wasn't going to say it. She plastered a smile on her face, or hoped she did. 'Good morning, Dr Alexander.' She heard the tremulous note in her voice, but hoped he hadn't noticed. 'I don't suppose I have to ask if you remember me?' It was an attempt at levity, and it flopped miserably.

'Hardly.' His voice was sarcastic, his green eyes as hard, cold, and impenetrable as granite. 'It was a memorable meal.'

'Yes, it was that,' she said, still feigning a lightness she didn't feel, 'and it wasn't exactly my finest hour as a waitress.' When he said nothing, but only looked at her with those cold, clear eyes, she ploughed courageously on. 'This is my brother, Clint Fraser, the park ranger you've been corresponding with.'

'Your *brother*! Then you're——' Jon Alexander came to an abrupt halt as his mind finally put two and two together. Of course—how stupid could he be? How many botany students would there be in a place like this? He should have realised it last night, especially when all those irrepressible and surprising thoughts about her kept popping into his mind with disconcerting regularity.

Holly shifted uncomfortably under a re-run of the Black Lagoon look, and was startled to discover how profoundly distressed she was by his hostility. And it was, she realised uneasily, a distress that had little to do with internships and school expenses.

Seeing that both his sister and Alexander were at a loss for words Clint stepped into the breach. 'Yes, Holly's your guide,' he said in his friendly, forthright way, 'and I assure you that her waitressing misadventures have nothing to do with her knowledge of mycology. There isn't a more competent local expert, not by a long shot.'

'Competent!' Jon Alexander scoffed, his voice dripping acid. 'I'd have a hard time believing she's competent enough to locate a mushroom in a grocery store, much less in a rain forest.'

Holly's cheeks flamed red as she dropped her eyes to the ground. Not in her whole life had anyone ever said anything so humiliating to her. Her stomach convulsed sickeningly, and then in a flash, the humiliation turned to seething, boiling anger. How *dared* he talk to her that way?

She opened her mouth to speak but Clint took a

swift, unobtrusive step forward and shot a raised-eyebrow glance at her that said: *You be quiet, little sister, and let me handle this. No nonsense, now*! It couldn't have been clearer if he'd spoke the words.

For a fraction of a second she came close to telling *him* off too, but then realised he was right. In the state she was in, if she tried to respond to Jon Alexander's contemptuous, maddeningly overbearing manner, she was likely to end up telling him exactly what she thought of him. A brilliant scientist he might be, but as a person, he certainly left a great deal to be desired. Arrogant, rude, and conceited were just some of the qualities that jumped all too readily to mind. But, satisfying as it would be to tell him so, it wouldn't be worth the price. Not *yet*, at any rate.

'She's also the only mycologist in the area right now,' Clint went on with studied patience. Holly looked up to see that despite the placating tone, her brother's blue eyes were dancing with indignation. Fortunately for her, maturity and a responsible job had taught Clint to control that blistering temper of his, a temper that would be matched—no, Holly amended, flickering a glance at the assertive, masculine pugnacity of the scientist's jaw-line, more likely surpassed—by Jon Alexander's.

'I've done a little collecting myself, of course,' her brother was saying, 'but I couldn't lead you to one-tenth of the species she can.'

To say that Jon Alexander looked rather doubtful would have been the year's most memorable understatement. Ignoring her, he

looked stonily at the ranger. Logic was telling him
that he had nothing to worry about with this
capable-looking brother of hers along, and a
moment's analysis made it clear that he was over-
reacting. But no amount of analytical thinking
could dispel the reluctance and displeasure that he
knew were in his eyes as he turned his head and
finally met the young woman's surprisingly
unabashed glance.

'It doesn't seem,' he said without expression,
'that I have much choice. Welcome aboard, Miss
Fraser.'

Clint Fraser, recognizing the mutinous look that
was flaring up in his sister's eyes as Alexander
regarded her unsmilingly, moved quickly to hustle
her back into the Jeep estate.

'Remember the internship,' Clint murmured for
Holly's ears alone, as he held open the door.
'That's important, Holly.' He grinned suddenly. 'If
not for that, I'd probably belt him myself. Maybe
I will yet.'

'Don't be silly,' she whispered back, but her
brother's words and Mike's surreptitious wink
cooled her temper and restored her common sense.

She was going to get the chance to prove herself,
and that was all that counted. But as her
resentment faded, her perplexity grew. Jon
Alexander's reaction to her rather minor misdeeds
was pretty excessive, if you thought about it. After
all, she hadn't spilled that dinner in his lap on
purpose—and certainly he had no basis on which
to doubt her mycological qualifications. It was his
own lab technician who had chosen her.

She let her eyes travel in his direction only after he'd briefly acknowledged Mike's greeting and got into the passenger seat directly in front of her. But study the back of him as she might, his thick, unruly russet hair, his straight neck, and his broad, powerful shoulders told her nothing. Nothing that is, except that her senses still prickled peculiarly with awareness of him.

As they drove east on South Shore Road among Douglas fir, spruce, and hemlock, Holly breathed a sigh of relief when it started to rain. That meant, at least, that the conditions for collecting would be ideal. If, on the other hand, the clouds had broken up, the sunshine and heat could well have caused many of the mushrooms, which fruit at night, to collapse and become unusable by mid-morning. Had that actually happened, she might have been sorely tempted to give up botany altogether and take up something restful and predictable, sky diving, perhaps.

Cheered by the feeling that her luck was beginning to change, she forced her eyes away from the man who sat so stoically in front of her, and watched through the window as the woods thickened into true rain forest. As always, Holly felt as if she was entering an enchanted land, a story-book place that couldn't really exist. Everything was green, a rainbow of greens—kelly, olive, emerald, shamrock, myrtle. Lush drapes of clubmoss trailed thickly from the towering, giant trees, and on the ground a dense profusion of oxalis, ferns, vanilla leaf, foamflower, and mosses covered every inch of soil and overwhelmed fallen branches and logs as well.

The rain had subsided into a faint drizzle by the time they'd reached the deserted Graves Creek Campground. With a squelch of tyres on wet fir needles and fallen autumn leaves, Mike brought the Jeep to a halt in one of the cleared campsites.

'End of the road, folks,' he drawled as he turned off the ignition and pulled up with a crunch on the parking brake.

While he eased Ferny and Dipper out of the trailer, Holly and Clint unloaded the gear. Then, with Mike's help it was only the work of minutes to load up the horses. In the meantime Jon Alexander spread out their topographic route map on a nearby wooden picnic table.

'Fine,' he commented crisply, after a brief examination. He refolded the map. 'I suggest we hike in all the way to Lake Olson without stopping, Miss Fraser. We'll start our collecting this afternoon after we get there.'

Holly was not misled by the polite wording. His authoritative tone translated 'I suggest' into a very clear 'We will.'

'Certainly, Dr Alexander,' she said, smiling frostily at him. 'Whatever you wish.' She was more than ready to match him formality for icy formality, if that's what he wanted. Even if it did strike a jarringly discordant note in this lush wilderness where easy going casualness was the time-honoured practice. 'There's a bit of a climb in places, but we should reach the lake by mid-afternoon—it's only a little over twelve miles.'

Although she was a long-legged five feet eight, her stride was shorter than the others', so Holly led the way down the trail alongside Graves Creek, setting the pace. The men followed single file, with Mike and the horses bringing up the rear.

The soothing, low burble of the creek as it tumbled over boulders and jagged rocks masked the sounds of footsteps behind her, and she quickly fell into a hiker's steady, swinging stride. Ordinarily, it would be only a matter of minutes before this almost primeval rain forest worked its magic on her, freeing her of any worries or irritations she'd brought to it. For this was no frightening, jungly swamp filled with deadly snakes and poisonous insects, as were the rain forests of the southern hemisphere, but a benign, friendly place, cool, restful, and soothing. There were dangers, of course, as in any wilderness, but you could pretty well relax and let your mind wander. The bears wouldn't bother you if you didn't bother them, and nothing worse than a mosquito was likely to sneak up behind you and take a bite out of you. And for that matter, there were hardly any mosquitoes.

The thick canopy of tree branches that arched over the rough, narrow trail completely blocked the sky for hundreds of yards at a time, giving the very air a blue-green, under-the-sea quality. Often she had let this illusion flow over her, imagining that she was walking on the bottom of a fairyland ocean of misty, dappled green. But today the disturbing element of Jon Alexander's presence did not encourage illusions.

To think she'd been breathlessly looking forward to this day since she'd first learned that a

serious research botanist had established his own
Institute on the other side of the mountain range.
And now, not only was she devastated over the
results of her meeting with the man whose sky-
rocketing career she'd followed so avidly, she felt
downright bereft. For over two years—ever since
his book had come out and she'd learnt some
details about his work—he'd served as a model for
her of what a scientist ought to be. Her cheeks
grew warm at the thought of all the times she'd
prattled to Anne about what a marvellous human
being he must be.

Well, she could still admire him for the fact that
the goals of his research were totally humani-
tarian—to help relieve world hunger—and not for
personal or commercial gain. But there was
nothing to admire, nothing to respect, in his
blatant insensitivity to other people's feelings.
Maybe he was one of those scientists who only
cared about people in the abstract. Maybe when
he was out of his laboratory and confronted with a
real, breathing person of flesh and blood, he was
as cold and unfeeling as a fish—his mercurial
temper notwithstanding. What else could explain
his behaviour? Talk about idols with feet of clay!
Only the flaw in this particular idol wasn't clay, it
was stone. And it wasn't in his feet, it was in that
heart of his: solid granite. Holly angrily snapped a
leaf from a bush as she passed it, refusing to listen
to a small voice inside her that said that flaws,
after all, are the only things that make idols
human. Striding more firmly, she managed to
quash this strangely upsetting thought. Somehow,

it made her acutely uncomfortable to think about Jon Alexander as a man and not as a scientist.

With only a short stop for lunch, they arrived at the lake by mid-afternoon as expected. Although the drizzle had ceased, pearly, translucent clouds covered the sky and kept the air cool, moist, invigorating, and perfect for collecting. So they stopped only long enough to select a campsite, stake the horses out to graze in a small grassy clearing nearby, and consume some chocolate for quick energy. Then, armed with one of the large, rubber-lined baskets and an assortment of other collecting paraphernalia, they set out foraging.

Time passed quickly. During the few remaining hours of daylight Holly managed with unerring accuracy to ferret out exactly the kinds of plants Jon Alexander was looking for. Experience told her just which species would be found in the open meadow, which on the trees, which on fallen branches, and which under rotting leaves. He was interested in all of them, but what engrossed him most were the little-known, beneficial organisms that coated shallow roots buried in the soft forest floor.

The basket was nearly full, as were the assortment of tins and glass tubes they'd brought along for the small specimens, when he called a halt.

'I need to expand some of my notes before going any further,' he announced, snapping closed his field notebook.

'It's about time to call it quits anyway,' Clint said, glancing at his watch, 'if we want to have enough light—not to mention energy—to set up camp and gather some firewood.'

'If you'd like,' Holly said to her brother and Mike when they reached the campsite, 'I'll go and look for some edible mushrooms that we can use as a garnish on those freeze-dried pork chops.'

At their ready assent, she walked along the shore of the lake until she spied a narrow break in the dense undergrowth that would allow her entrance into a thick stand of tall Douglas fir. Tucked under a thicket of blueberry bushes that grew at the base of several nearby trees, and almost hidden by fallen fir needles, she found a clump of several dozen chanterelles, the most delectable of wild mushrooms.

Brushing away the fragrant needles, Holly knelt and gathered the delicate golden mushrooms, placing them in a plastic bag. There were more than enough for the four of them. She retraced her steps back to the lake, to discover Jon Alexander striding down the shoreline in her direction, frowning and abstracted. Carrying an oversized clipboard and his notebook, he was obviously in search of a quiet spot to think, away from the wood-chopping and stake-hammering of the camp.

Holly took a step back, preparing to fade into the foliage; she had no desire to exchange even a casual remark with him—not without the comforting presence of a third party. At that moment he lifted his eyes from the ground and saw her. His frown deepened, which hardly surprised her. All afternoon he'd remained stubbornly glacial and aloof, despite the inarguably expert work she'd done.

Dismissing as undignified an impulse to scurry off into the bushes like a startled mouse at the sight of a hawk, Holly forced herself to move forward.

As they neared each other, he noticed the full plastic bag, and glowering disapproval leapt into his green eyes. 'If those are for dinner, let's hope you haven't got a death cap or two in there,' he said cuttingly.

That did it! Drawing in an angry breath, Holly shot him what she hoped was a withering look. 'Must you be so needlessly offensive?' she snapped. 'Is it simply that you enjoy it?'

Without waiting for an answer and with tears not far from the surface she brushed past him. She could take that arrogant, insufferable manner of his if she had to, but she was darned if she was meekly going to accept any more of his insults. The chanterelle mushrooms she'd just gathered were quite distinctive in shape and colour—a rich yellow, wildly different from the poisonous death caps. Even a novice could tell them apart—as he very well knew!

She'd gone only a few yards when a firm, masculine hand stopped her.

'Let go of me.' Her luminous blue eyes flashed as she turned towards him.

His grip on her arm tightened. 'Not until you listen to me for a moment,' he said abruptly.

If Holly hadn't been so dazed by the way his touch heightened those strange, unsettling sensations she felt whenever he was near her, her blood pressure would have shot up another notch in response to his infuriatingly dictatorial tone.

'I owe you an apology,' he said unexpectedly. The sincerity in his voice jolted her out of her anger; she could feel it evaporate like dew in the sunlight. Even his face had changed, discarding the cold, aloof mask it had worn from the moment she'd first seen him. And he was smiling . . . at her! Not the warmest grin she'd ever seen, but an honest-to-goodness smile all the same.

'What I said back there was completely uncalled-for,' he continued. Seeing she wasn't going to run off he dropped his hand from her arm. 'I guess I've been in a snappish mood, but that's my problem, not yours—or it ought to be. Your field knowledge of mycology is first rate. I couldn't have a better guide.' He shrugged, as if uneasy giving praise, 'I just thought I ought to tell you.'

The band that had been constricting her chest since the night before gave way, even if the warmth of his expression failed to light those cool green eyes. They were as guarded and inscrutable as ever. But the open hostility was gone and she was inclined to be grateful for small favours.

'Thanks for saying that,' she said, smiling tentatively back at him, unable to hide the relief in her voice. 'I suppose we just got off on the wrong foot . . . And I really am sorry about last night, Dr Alexander. I'm not usually so clumsy. Honestly.'

His smile turned mildly rueful, even charming, and his eyes actually warmed just a little. The change in his expression wasn't very great, and yet it seemed to catch at the breath in her throat.

'Nothing's gone wrong all day, so I'm inclined

to believe you just had a bad night. As a matter of fact,' he said, as a new, unreadable expression flitted briefly over his masculine, strongly-defined features, 'I didn't have such a good one myself. Anyway, do accept my apologies.'

That apparently ended the royal interview, and she stood for a moment looking at his ramrod-straight back as he walked past her without a backward glance. So his heart wasn't solid granite after all, just encased in it. Never had she been exposed to a person with so many layers ... so mystifyingly complex ... so difficult to read. And whether she liked it or not, circumstances had thrust him into her life as a force to be reckoned with. The thought should have intrigued and challenged her, yet all she felt was a disquieting, timorous fear. How silly! Where was her backbone, for goodness sake?

Resolutely, Holly tore her eyes away from the distant, retreating figure and walked quickly back to camp.

CHAPTER THREE

IT was Clint who first noticed the cloud mass building up in the west when they stopped in a small clearing at mid-morning. 'That's surprising. I didn't think another storm front was due until Thursday.'

'Well, we can certainly use some moisture.' Holly brushed a few strands of hair from her forehead as she studied the clouds. 'Maybe there'll be a shower this afternoon,' she said hopefully.

'Doesn't look heavy enough,' Clint replied, plopping himself down on a lichen-covered rock. 'But at least things will cool off and you can stop running yourself ragged, sis. Let's take a break.'

Holly glanced several yards downstream to where Jon Alexander was busy with his field notebook, jotting down relevant details about the mushrooms they'd just discovered. She was happy to see that he'd yet to prepare separate identification labels to be tucked in with each one. That meant he'd be busy for at least another five or ten minutes and she could have a breather. Gratefully, she selected her own rock and followed her brother's example.

Ever since she'd crawled out of her sleeping-bag to discover that the day was dawning clear, bright, and warm, she'd been working frantically to locate and collect as many species of mushroom as she

could before the heat collapsed or damaged them.
She was more than ready for a break, and she was
ravenous too. Breakfast—cold cereal hurriedly
consumed while standing—hadn't been any too
substantial to begin with, and it seemed as if
they'd had it ages and ages ago.

'I don't suppose either of you thought to bring
some granola bars along?' she asked wistfully.

'I wish we had,' Mike groaned, letting himself
fall back against a fallen tree trunk, massive and
comfortable-looking. It was a mistake. The solid-
seeming, waist-high trunk squashed under him like
wet tissue paper, collapsing in a pulpy mess to the
forest floor. It was not an uncommon phenomenon
in the rain forest, where sturdy-looking, moss-
covered exteriors often hid interiors that had long
ago rotted away to nothing. But it always caught
one by surprise.

'Damn,' Mike swore, tumbling down on to his
heels and elbows.

The good-natured laughter bubbling up in Holly
and her brother died as they saw Mike's mouth
twist in pain. 'My foot ...' he said through
clenched teeth.

They reached him quickly with Jon Alexander
not far behind. He and Clint eased Mike into a
sitting position on the ground, and the ranger
unlaced his left boot with gentle hands. Without
taking it off, he ran his fingers along his ankle.

'It doesn't feel broken,' Clint said. 'Does it still
hurt?'

'Yeah, it hurts,' Mike admitted sheepishly.

'He could have cracked his heel bone,' Jon

Alexander interjected, 'which is just as bad. I'd advise leaving his shoe on, and putting on a splint.'

Clint sat back on his heels. 'I think you're right,' he said, 'and then we'll have to get him out of here. Will you look around for something we can use as a splint?' He turned to his sister. 'Holly, you come back to camp with me. You can get some food together while I get the horses ready.'

Fortunately they'd been circling as they collected, so that the accident had occurred less than a mile from camp. Within the hour they had Mike's lower leg immobilised and had him up, reasonably securely, on Ferny. Mike was gamely joking about his clumsiness, but the skin around his mouth was grey, and his forehead shone with tiny beads of sweat.

'There's no sense in your hiking out with us,' Clint said to Holly. He included the scientist in his glance. 'You'd only slow us down, so you might as well go on working.' Looking at his watch, he added, 'I'll get Mike back to Lake Quinault and have Mary take him to the doctor, then start back straight away. With fresh horses, I shouldn't have any trouble making it back here before dark.'

Clint's plan was too sensible for anyone to disagree, but Holly could see that Jon Alexander was far from happy as the two men, astride the horses, slowly disappeared down the trail.

A faint frown creased his forehead. 'Well, we might as well get back to work,' he said in a tone that was several degrees cooler than the one he'd been using since his surprising apology.

A tinge of colour mantled Holly's cheeks as she nodded her assent. How embarrassing! For some reason or other the man clearly didn't want to be alone with her. Obviously, their truce was over; she was back on the receiving end of the cold-shoulder treatment. And it felt awful. She was surprised at the sudden rush of resentment against this man with the awesome power of making her happy or miserable with a few words or a casual glance.

Angry and upset with him, but far too proud to try to cajole him back into a good mood, Holly morosely picked up one of the wicker baskets and wordlessly started foraging upstream.

The afternoon was well along when he finally called a halt.

'I'd like to save some room for more lower-elevation samples,' he said wrapping a prime specimen of lion's mane in waxed paper and setting it carefully in a basket. Then, in what Holly felt was a distinctly grudging tone of admiration, he added, 'Thanks to those identification skills of yours, storage space could get to be a problem.'

At least, she thought as they turned back towards Lake Olson, the business part of the field trip was turning out to be a success. Not that anything else was. Even the weather began turning against them as they started for camp. The clouds, which had been fluffy white earlier, and which she'd hoped would bring mists and showers, had dulled to a malevolent, gun-metal grey, and in the distance was the rumble of thunder, quickly coming closer as they walked.

'That's funny,' Holly said, casting a worried look at the lowering sky. 'We don't usually get heavy storms at this time of year.' As if to refute her words a jagged flash of lightning lit up the dark underside of the clouds, to be followed almost immediately by a sizzling clap of thunder near at hand.

'I think this may be an exception,' he rejoined drily. 'We'd better put on our ponchos.'

It was a good thing they did. The heavy, slanting downpour caught them just as they reached the camp.

'Your brother would be crazy to try to make it back in this,' Jon Alexander said gloomily, as they ducked under the shelter of the cooking tarpaulin. 'He'd drown.'

'I agree with you,' Holly said. 'He's got good sense, though. He'll just hole up in the Jeep at the Graves Creek trailhead, until it blows over.'

'Probably,' he said. 'But what if he doesn't? What if he's worried about us and tries to make it back here, and gets stuck half-way along the trail? No, I'm concerned about him; we'd better get going ourselves, and try to meet up with him.'

It was on the tip of Holly's tongue to tell him her brother could take care of himself—he was a forest ranger, after all—when it finally dawned on her that what Jon Alexander feared was the prospect of spending the night alone with her. At first she almost laughed. Wasn't it supposed to be the other way round? On second thoughts, it wasn't very funny at all. Did he think she was the sort of woman who would make a pass at him?

And did he find her so unattractive that the thought repelled him? Either way, she resented it. Glad that her cheeks were already red from the bitingly cold wind, Holly nodded her head. 'All right,' she murmured, not looking at him, 'we'll head back towards Graves Creek.'

'We'll eat first,' he decided—without asking her, naturally—'then go. We'll store the equipment here and we can leave the specimens. They're all packed securely, and in this weather they'll do fine until we can come back for them tomorrow.'

'Fine,' she said shortly.

He looked up sharply at the tone in her voice. 'Something the matter?'

'Nothing—except that to be on the safe side we ought to take our sleeping-bags and tents with us—just in case we don't make it all the way back to the trailhead and we have to spend the night in the forest.'

He looked at her as if she'd just told him that all there was to eat were boiled worms and fried toads.

'All right,' he said at last, his voice expressionless. 'We'll take them along.'

The storm was fierce and noisy, with screaming wind, crackling lightning, and great booming rolls of thunder that seemed to vibrate the very earth beneath them. Nevertheless, Holly moved swiftly and confidently along the trail, even in the deepening darkness. She had been in enough such rain-forest storms to know they sounded far more savage than they were. The towering trees and thick, tall brush kept the worst of the wind and water from them, and with heavy-duty, hooded ponchos that kept everything but their faces as dry as toast, and powerful, battery-operated torches, they made good time.

Besides, she was now just as anxious to get out of the rain forest and away from the presence of the infuriating man slogging behind her as he was to be done with her. Famous botanists . . .! She would be quite content if she never met another one.

She quickened her pace, pausing only briefly when the trail degenerated to a series of stepping-stones and boulders across Graves Creek. She was surprised to see that the water level had risen to cover many of the stones with a thin, slippery sheen.

'Stay where you are,' he ordered imperiously. 'I'll cross first and toss you a rope. The footing's going to be tricky.'

In response, she jumped nimbly to the first boulder. If he thought she needed his help—she, who had practically grown up in the rain forest—then he had another think coming. 'It's not the least bit necessary,' she called back from her perch, her chin tilted defiantly. 'I've crossed this stream a hundred times, in all kinds of weather, and I'm perfectly capable of crossing it now, without your help, thank you.' She didn't bother telling him that she had never seen the creek this swollen, but that was none of his business.

On that note, she hopped to the next rock, but more intent on demonstrating her agility than on being careful, she lost her footing on the slimy, wet, moss-covered surface. She teetered wildly, arms rotating like windmills, trying desperately to regain her balance, refusing to believe that this was really happening. From the corner of her eye she could see a calm, interested Jon Alexander observing her with what could only be called a sneer on his arrogant face.

She almost—just almost—made it, but then, with a squelchy, sodden skid, her feet shot out from under her and she tumbled into the creek with a splash that sounded like Niagara Falls. For one long, mortifying moment she just sat there, poncho fanning out behind her in the stream and icy water up to her shoulders. She almost wished it had been deep enough to drown in, because anything was better than sitting there like a great lump, bedraggled and freezing, under Jon Alexander's detached, maddeningly amused gaze. He thought it was funny! And his expression showed it. No longer wary of her, at least for the moment, he was obviously entertained. That aloof mask was off again, and with his eyes twinkling and his lips struggling against laughter, there was a lovely, boyish appeal in his face. But all things considered, she wished he'd retreat back behind the mask again. For that matter she wished he'd just retreat, full stop . . . go away . . . leave her to her mortification in peace.

With his hands on his hips, he surveyed her with open contempt. One eyebrow rose lazily, and he opened his mouth to speak.

'One word!' Holly warned fiercely. 'Just say one

word, and, so help me, I'll ... I'll scream ... I'll ...' She stood up, tongue-tied, water cascading from her.

'Do I gather that you're implying this is my fault?' he responded imperturbably.

'Yes!' she snapped angrily. 'Yes! It's all your fault. This and everything else, for that matter—including my dropping your dinner!' She waded to the far side. 'And I'm glad it landed in your stupid lap!'

He crossed agilely over the rocks and boulders—without even coming close to slipping, damn him—and joined her.

Holly's bright blue eyes blazed. 'It's your fault,' she cried again, her pent-up emotions spilling over, 'because you're without a doubt the rudest, most overbearing, most despicable man I've ever met—or even heard of!'

'And my being rude—not to mention despicable—is what makes you clumsy,' he taunted mockingly, his eyes full of sardonic humour. 'Hmm, that's quite interesting.'

Now he *was* laughing at her!

'*Yes!* If I hadn't thought so highly of you—not that I do any more, I assure you—I wouldn't have been so nervous ... so ridiculously anxious to please you.' She flung the words at him. 'Well, now I know better, thank goodness.'

'Oh, I see.' The unflappable condescension in his voice and the glittering mockery in those grey-green eyes made her blood boil 'Well,' he continued, 'I think we'd better finish this discussion after you get some dry clothes on. Thank God your backpack is waterproof.'

He pointed to a relatively dry spot under a mossy rock overhang a few yards from the creek. 'That's as good a spot as any to change your clothes. I'll turn round.'

Holly didn't like the idea of following his instructions, but he was right. It was as wet on the inside of the poncho as on the outside. Head high, she stalked to the overhang and, once she was somewhat sheltered from the rain she drew her poncho over her head, then shrugged out of her backpack. Her bravado lasted her only as a long as it took to get a good look at the pack. Somehow, inexcusably, she hadn't zipped the top all the way closed. Her face fell as she saw the results. Water had flooded in, thoroughly soaking her one extra set of clothes. With her heart thumping, she untied the bright blue slipcover that protected her sleeping-bag and reached in. Her nervous, chilled fingers closed on water-sodden material and she groaned aloud. The cover was water-resistant, not waterproof. There was a big difference, and her bag had got drenched while she had sat stupidly paralysed with embarrassment in the stream. How completely idiotic of her. Not that trying to show off by bounding gazelle-like across the stream had been exactly brilliant either.

'What's the matter?' he called. When she didn't answer, he turned around to see her staring dejectedly at her gear.

Matter? Holly thought. Nothing, absolutely nothing at all. She'd merely lost an internship and to top it off she was probably going to expire of pneumonia! Aside from that, everything was fine.

When he reached her side she kept her face averted. If he laughed at her again, she'd hit him. No, she didn't have the fight for that any more. She'd probably just burst into tears.

He took the situation in with a glance. 'I suppose this is my fault too?'

'No,' she muttered dully, through teeth that were beginning to chatter with cold. 'It's my own carelessness.'

He quickly shrugged off his backpack. 'I've got a wool shirt and some socks that I want you to put on,' he ordered firmly. 'Right now. I'll set up my tent between those two small trees and lay out my sleeping-bag. Then I want you to get into it and warm up.'

'What will you do?'

'I'm going to gather some firewood. There's still some daylight left, if you can call this daylight, and if we can get a fire going in here we should be able to dry out your clothes in a few hours and then go on.'

'Okay,' Holly answered meekly, surprised that he hadn't ranted and raved about her block-headedness. *This* time she deserved some ranting.

She was shivering badly by the time she'd peeled off her wet clothes, unplaited her thick hair so it could dry, and dived into his sleeping-bag, but within minutes she was beginning to thaw. Snuggled comfortably, she listened for his sounds outside, but couldn't hear anything beyond the wild drumming of rain on the canvas just a few feet above her, and the occasional booming echo of thunder. With weather like this, Clint was sure to

spend the night in the Jeep, never dreaming that
they'd be foolish enough to leave camp.

Jon Alexander's sleeping-bag was wonderfully
roomy and warm, and redolent of his faint,
cedary, cleanly masculine scent. With a sigh, she
burrowed more deeply into it. Her eyelids began to
grow heavy . . .

An icy, wet breeze on her face jolted her
abruptly awake. He was in the tent with her. At
least he had stuck his head and shoulders through
the opening. Holly rose up on one elbow. The
craggy, strong planes of his face, glistening with
rain, were lit up dramatically by his torch, so that
he looked more virile, more powerful than ever.
She was clothed modestly enough in his green-and-
tan woollen shirt, but she was far too conscious of
the fact that she had nothing on underneath. But
then, she had to admit that semi-clothed females
seemed like the last thing Dr Jon Alexander had
on his mind . . . or at any rate, a semi-clothed
female named Holly Fraser.

'Where did you put the tube of Fire Ribbon?' he
asked brusquely, brushing at the rain that
streamed down his face in rivulets.

'Fire Ribbon?' she echoed. She remembered
packing it . . . but where?

'Yes, the Fire Ribbon,' he said drily. As if he were
speaking to a particularly dense child, he added.
'You know, that nifty substance without which it is
somewhat difficult to start a fire with wet wood?'

She flushed. 'I . . . Suddenly it came to her.
She'd put it in Clint's backpack—which was with
the rest of their things at Lake Olson. 'Oh, no,' she

moaned, 'I left it behind!'

He raised his eyes heavenwards. 'Of all the idiotic . . . this takes the cake!'

'I didn't do it on pur——'

'Spare me,' he grated in exasperation. 'We'll have to spend the night here.'

'We *can't*,' she said, in a stifled voice, her heart thudding. 'It's pouring, and there's only one dry sleeping-bag—*this* one!'

'Which we'll have to share,' he said, grimacing.

'*Share!*' It made her head reel just to think about it. She pulled the bag closer about her. 'Why, I'd rather get pneumonia! I'd never——'

'Suit yourself,' Jon Alexander interrupted grimly, 'because I damn well don't have any intentions of getting it myself.' He set the torch down inside and pulled his head back outside. She could hear him taking off his poncho. Shielding himself with it from the driving rain, he scrambled into the small tent on his knees.

Holly tried to pull herself and the sleeping-bag as far from him as she could, which wasn't far. Technically, it was a two-man tube tent, but the manufacturer hadn't had anybody as big as Jon Alexander in mind.

'Really, you can't sleep in here with me,' she gasped. Trying one last tactic, she argued, 'It's . . . it's ungentlemanly.'

He went on busily unlacing his boots. 'Ungentlemanly? Haven't you ever heard of the equal rights movement?'

She gulped. 'But—I mean, I barely have anything on!'

With no response but an irritated sigh he leaned over and tugged at the zipper pull on the sleeping-bag.

Good heavens, he was really going to do it! Holly nearly made a panicked grab for the zipper herself, but against his strength what would have been the use? Mutely, she watched him, her eyes as big as saucers, her heart in her mouth.

With the zipper half-way down he paused, looking at her, his exasperation momentarily softened by the colour flooding her cheeks, the trepidation in her eyes. My God, she *was* an innocent! Still, this was clearly the only sensible thing to do—and it was her fault after all.

'If you're worried about rape,' he said, 'don't be. We've been on our feet since dawn. I'm tired, I'm wet, and I'm cold. And even if I weren't,' he added derisively, 'I avoid idiotic little schoolgirls the way I'd avoid bubonic plague. And that's putting it mildly!'

Holly tossed her head in indignation. Her lustrous hair fanned out, grazing his shoulder and he drew back as if scorched. Somehow, that instinctive reaction affronted her more than his words had.

'I happen to be twenty-one and a senior at college. I'm not a schoolgirl, I assure you!'

'I'm impressed,' he said with exaggerated sarcasm, his green eyes unreadable. 'Do I take that as an invitation?' The razor-sharp edge to his voice was infuriating.

Her cheeks grew redder. 'Of *course* not! That's not what I meant at all——'

'Then what *do* you mean?'

As if she knew herself. One thing she did know was that she didn't care a bit for Jon Alexander's disdainful dismissal of her as a desirable woman. Yet on the other hand, she detested him. So what did it matter? Damn him, nothing seemed simple any more.

'I don't know what I meant,' she said, her voice quivering, as she rolled over on her side, 'except you made it sound like I was in the fourth form or something.'

'With your brains,' he muttered scathingly, 'it's a wonder you ever got out of the third form.'

That didn't deserve to be dignified with an answer, and Holly contented herself with throwing him a look over her shoulder that should have shrivelled him on the spot. It didn't.

He ignored her and reached over to flip off the torch. In the dark he slid beside her. She didn't know quite what she expected to feel when he did, but she found herself somehow shocked at the warmth of his long body, of his . . . aliveness. Had she expected a statue? She didn't have much time to think about it, because he quickly shifted to provide as much space as possible between them, which was a relief . . . she thought. Then he turned his broad back to her and sighed—in annoyance? Weariness? And was still. Although the rain blocked out sounds of breathing, he lay so quietly that she could only assume he had fallen asleep at once.

In no way, though, was she going to be able to sleep even for a few minutes. Not with a strange man in her bed, so to speak. (Come to think of it, never mind the 'so to speak'.) When it came to the romantic part of life, Holly knew that she was definitely backward for her years. Jon Alexander, clearly experienced in such matters, had probably known it as soon as he saw her. In that sense, he had a point in calling her a schoolgirl. She was still in kindergarten, never mind the third form.

Holly had never been in love, not unless you counted that crush on Mr Kerner, her history teacher, when she was fourteen. And she'd never been in bed with a man. (Not before tonight!) That was hardly surprising, since she couldn't imagine having an affair with someone she didn't love. What there was in her background that had given her that out-of-vogue morality she didn't know, but there it was, and she wouldn't have changed it if she could. Which she couldn't.

There had been more than her old-fashioned virtue to protect her; there had been Clint. When a girl lives in a small community where everyone knows everyone else, and she has a very big, very husky, very hot-headed older brother, she is unlikely to be the object of too many passes. Not that Clint was a violent person, of course, but no one doubted that he'd put a dent or two in the anatomy of anyone who exceeded the bounds of propriety with his little sister.

But those weren't the real reasons for her innocence at twenty-one, and deep down Holly knew it. Big brothers can be avoided and people come up with all kinds of ways to win arguments against their morals, given enough motivation.

The real reason, the deep reason, was far more simple, so basic that the whole question of affairs was academic. For Holly Fraser, in all her years, had never met a man who stirred the least flutter, the vaguest inkling, of a physical spark in her. It was, in fact, something that had made her wonder from time to time, if there wasn't something missing in her chemistry.

Well, she didn't have to wonder any more, because the frustrating, unreadable man beside her made every atom in her body quiver if he just looked at her. Not that it mattered, a more unlikely lover she couldn't imagine, and for more than one reason—not the least of which was that they seemed to spend most of their time glaring stiffly at one another like a couple of angry cats in an uneasy stand-off.

And yet, whatever the reason, she wasn't angry now, even with him there like that, and she wasn't quivering either—not exactly. What she was, was sleepy. Sleepy and secure, as odd as it seemed.

As Holly's mind wandered on, she felt her muscles relax involuntarily. It was lovely to be warm and dry, and listening to the steady drumming of the rain pelting ineffectually at the tent roof over them. Warm and safe. Curious to feel so safe, but she did. There was his broad, muscular back just six inches from her, barely visible in the darkness, a protective shield between her and the streaming, black wilderness outside. Smiling at the thought, she fell asleep.

She woke from a most unsettling and novel dream

because something heavy seemed to be on her
chest. It took her disorganised mind a moment to
discover just what it was. Jon Alexander was
sprawled half across her, dead to the world, his
head on her breasts and one leg thrown over hers.
She lay very still. The unravelling threads of the
appallingly sensual dream about him still hung
hazily about her, and she had no desire to wake
him until she could compose herself, mind and
body. And there was even more that needed
composing. Somehow, during the restless night,
the top few buttons of her shirt had come undone.
Perhaps if she continued to lie very quietly he'd
eventually move in his sleep and give her a chance
to button up before he saw her. If not for that, she
told herself, she'd certainly wake him up at once
and tell him to remove himself.

Indeed, he did stir without opening his eyes, but
to her dismay he resettled his cheek against her
bare flesh, in the valley between her breasts, his
lips sleepily nuzzling her velvety skin. She bit back
a gasp. What was she going to do if he woke up
now?

Her eyes widened when his hand moved up,
and when it curved around the soft mound of her
breast, it sent shivers racing so unexpectedly and
explosively through her nervous system that her
breath caught in her throat.

He moved slightly again—more shivers—and
murmured something with his eyes closed. 'Mmm,
nice,' she was sure it was! How embarrassing!
Obviously, he thought he was waking up to some
woman in his past ... or present, for all she

knew. For an irrational moment jealousy flared and blazed up in her. *Jealousy* ... she must be going crazy!

Finally she managed to clear her throat and speak, after a fashion. 'Um ... Dr Alexander, could you ... uh ...' She stifled a sudden, near-hysterical giggle. Considering the circumstances, 'Dr Alexander' was just a little on the formal side.

He was instantly awake, but it took his eyes a second to focus. When they did, it was as if someone had emptied a bucket of icy water on him. His head jerked up and his hand pulled convulsively back. 'Good Lord ...!' He seemed to choke on his words, and Holly heard him swallow with some difficulty. What was *he* so upset about? *She* was the one in the humiliating situation.

What she couldn't know, of course, was what a breathtaking vision of heartbreakingly innocent seductiveness he was looking at. The muted, pale light of dawn penetrating the tent lit the heavy, tousled masses of raven-black hair that spilled in sensual waves around her face, and cast a soft golden spotlight on her small, perfect breasts, camellia-white except for their upraised rosy tips, just visible in the disarranged, wide-open neck of the plaid shirt.

He tore his eyes away and looked down on that lovely face—now pale and alarmed—the soft lips parted in confusion ... and again, unwillingly, his eyes slid to her gleaming breasts. With more rock-hard discipline than he'd ever needed in his life—for anything—he turned his face away, trembling deep inside him, aching to press his mouth against those kissable lips, those sweet breasts, to simply take her, and damn the consequences. Not that it would need any force. All too clearly, she was already half-aroused, whether she knew it or not. All he had to do . . .

He wrenched his mind away from the overpowering images. 'Why the hell didn't you wake me before this?' he grated.

'I . . . I . . .' The harsh ferocity of his voice, the angry tension in his body seemed to shock her out of her trance. She'd lain there, unable to move, held by the towering intensity of his gaze, the seething tension that had made his eyes seem to glow with a fierce, savage light.

'And for Christ's sake, close that shirt!'

The blood was suddenly hot in her cheeks. Her hands fumbled up and clutched the shirt together as sheer rage at the injustice of it all finally loosened her tongue.

'You're horrible!' she blazed. 'You're a beast, and I hope with all my heart I never see you again! *Ever!*'

'That suits me fine!' he retorted caustically, and stormed out of the tent.

Thirty seconds later the tent flap was yanked back and Holly's damp jeans came sailing in to flop in a crumpled heap at the foot of the sleeping bag. That, followed by the sounds of tent stakes being yanked up around her, told Holly that Jon Alexander was wasting no time in getting under way. And good riddance.

Grimacing at the contact of the clammy denim against her overheated flesh, she scrambled into her jeans, barely making it outside before he released the mainstay and the tent collapsed.

Her eyes sparkling with temper, she informed him haughtily, 'I don't need the map, you can take——'

'We're hiking out together,' he cut in.

'No way,' she bristled back furiously. 'I wouldn't walk two yards with you if my life depended on it!'

Jon Alexander stopped rolling up his bag and looked up, his face darkening ominously. Eye to eye, they glared at each other.

'Either you come under your own steam or I'll carry you like a sack of potatoes,' he said, and the look in his flinty grey-green eyes told her that he meant it. Impotent anger flooded through her. His sense of responsibility was nothing more than rank chauvinism—chauvinism backed up by sheer brute strength. Damn him!

'And if I were you,' he continued in a voice dripping with sarcasm, 'I'd take the former option. At least that'll give me a chance to think up some diplomatic excuse to give your brother about regrettably having to call a sudden halt to this fascinating field trip. Once we're out of here you'll be free to go your merry little way wreaking havoc elsewhere, and I can get on with my work ... peacefully.'

He couldn't have picked a better bribe to sway her into co-operating. The whole experience had been traumatic enough without having to go through the mortification of telling anyone—least of all Clint—about it. To avoid that she would have spent a few hours in the presence of the devil himself. Mutely acquiescent, she spun on her heel and stalked to the overhang to retrieve her shoes and backpack. The sooner they got out of here the better.

CHAPTER FOUR

DR ANGELA AUGUSTA KIRKLAND removed her reading glasses, picked up their case from the oak lectern, and slipped the glasses inside. 'I expect to have your workbooks graded and ready for you to pick up in the office by next Tuesday,' she said, signalling the end of the lab session. 'Next term will be devoted to individual research projects.' As the professor gathered her notes together, she added, 'I suggest you give some thought to the topic of your project during the spring break.'

The instant she concluded, the air filled with end-of-term noises: excited chatter, papers rustling, books slamming closed, chairs scraping back and drawers being firmly and enthusiastically banged shut.

'I'm not giving a thought to anything during vacation but sleeping in and sailing,' Anne vowed to Holly, bending over a storage drawer.

'Sailing?' Holly responded absent-mindedly, gathering together her dissection tools. 'With whom?'

'Jim Everett. And guess what?' Anne leaned conspiratorially closer. 'He's told me to invite you along, because he has a friend from Seattle who wants to meet you.' Coaxingly, she added, 'Jim says he's very attractive.'

Holly tucked her tools in the back of the

drawer. 'I don't think so, I——' She came to an abrupt stop as she saw the tall, erect form of Dr Kirkland approaching the workbench, and a mixture of guilt and stubbornness leapt into her blue eyes.

'Holly, I'd like to see you in my office as soon as possible,' Dr Kirkland ordered crisply.

'Yes, Dr Kirkland,' Holly replied in a subdued voice, suppressing a sigh. She knew quite well why her professor wanted to see her, and she wasn't looking forward to the interview. 'I'll be there as soon as I finish putting my things away.'

Anne waited until Dr Kirkland was out of earshot. 'I told you she wasn't going to let the application period lapse without knowing why you're not applying for the internship.'

'Well, I suppose you're right,' Holly said glumly.

'And if you don't mind me saying so,' Anne said, unplugging her microscope, 'you're being ridiculously mysterious about why you changed your mind about applying.'

A wry smile touched Holly's lips. 'Why should I mind your saying so, especially since this is about the fiftieth time you have—making an average of twice a week for six months.'

Anne was not to be deterred. 'Okay, so I've mentioned it a few times. But honestly, Holly, I'm your closest friend—your roommate—how can I help worrying, when ever since September you've gone around in a blue funk? You've turned down practically every social invitation you've had, you've turned down dates——' Anne's impulsive, friendly voice was rising. She lowered it, real concern in her eyes. 'I know something awful must have happened, and I just think maybe you'd snap out of it if you only talked about it.'

'There's nothing to tell,' Holly said, not meeting her friend's eyes. 'Dr Alexander and I didn't hit it off, that's all. So it would be a waste of time for me to apply for the internship.' She shut the storage drawer with a firm snap, hoping she'd closed the subject as well. Anne was only trying to help, of course, but the last thing Holly wanted was to talk about it.

'Sorry, Holly dear, but I'm unconvinced,' Anne rejoined. She slipped a plastic dustcover over her microscope and pushed it to the back of the workbench. 'That's just not enough reason for you to lose that pre-Jon Alexander disposition you used to have, and I bet Kirkland doesn't swallow that line either.'

Knowing Anne was right, Holly tapped on Dr Kirkland's door with dread.

'Close the door behind you, Holly, and take a seat,' her instructor said, studying her with clear, intelligent eyes. Holly did as she was told, but perched on the edge of the chair, hoping for a getaway as soon as possible.

A silver-haired, gently austere woman in her late forties, Angela Kirkland made it a practice neither to discuss personal matters nor to socialise with her students. 'It has been my experience,' she had been heard to say, 'that authority diminishes in direct proportion as fraternisation increases.' About to break her own rule, she approached the subject cautiously.

'Perhaps you've forgotten that Monday is the last day you can apply for the Alexander internship?'

'No.' Keeping her eyes averted, Holly toyed nervously with her handbag strap. 'I'm not applying for it.'

'Not applying for it!' the older woman echoed. She'd sensed something was bothering her top student even though Holly's grades had remained consistently high. But she hadn't realised the situation was this serious.

Not a person to mince words, she said, 'But that's ridiculous. You have an extremely good chance of getting it.'

'I don't think so, Dr Kirkland. Not when it's Dr Alexander himself who's going to decide between the three top candidates.' Holly spoke matter-of-factly. Then, hoping eye contact would add veracity to her words she looked up and delivered to Dr Kirkland the same non-explanation she had been giving everyone. 'We just didn't hit it off. Personality differences, I guess.'

Her professor would have none of it. 'Nonsense. Whether or not you "hit it off," as you say, is immaterial. Neither of two previous interns has worked directly under Dr Alexander, you know. It's highly probable you'd never even see him.'

Holly bit her lip, guilt rising within her. Her instructors—particularly Dr Kirkland—had singled her out as a student worth their time and attention—extra time and attention. She owed them something for that, but wild horses wouldn't have been able to drag the whole story out of her. Still, some further explanation was called for.

Tentatively, she said, 'Well, it was more than not getting along. We . . . we had words.'

Dr Kirkland's brown eyes widened slightly. For her it was a dramatic display of emotion. She leaned back in her swivel chair and examined her student keenly for a moment. 'Words? That sounds a bit melodramatic, Holly. Isn't it possible that whatever happened has been blown up disproportionately in your mind?'

Holly tried a laugh, but it wasn't a success. 'If you only knew.'

Dr Kirkland touched the earpiece of her glasses reflectively to her lips. 'Holly,' she said firmly, 'I want you to tell me about it.'

Eyes downcast once again, Holly swallowed. Forcing herself to speak calmly, she gave a highly abbreviated account of the weekend, leaving out—never even coming near—the final humiliating scene in the tent. 'I suppose,' she said, by way of summing up, 'that I was so keyed up at the thought of actually working with him . . .' a touch of bitterness crept into her tone and she tried to dampen it '. . . that I became terribly clumsy and . . . and gauche.'

The silence that followed her recital seemed deafening, and Holly looked up to find her professor gazing musingly at her pen which she was twirling slowly in her long fingers.

Finally she looked up and spoke. 'Did you actually tell him how much you admired him?'

'Yes, in the restaurant,' Holly replied, smiling bleakly at the memory. 'You'd have thought I insulted him.'

Dr Kirkland sighed. 'Holly, I'm depending on your discretion not to repeat what I'm going to tell you ... It's an old, long-suppressed scandal that I'd hate to see come out into the open, even now—but I'm sure it explains his reaction to you.'

Holly felt a peculiar shiver run slowly down her spine. Did she really want to know anything that would rob her of her fierce resentment of Jon Alexander? *No*, came the automatic response; but she remained sitting in the chair as if glued to it.

Dr Kirkland took another deep breath. 'I can't go into detail without breaking a confidence, but early in his career he was an assistant professor at a university back east. In his second year of teaching he was found with a young female student in what appeared to be compromising circumstances. The evidence was damning, despite the fact that he firmly maintained his innocence, and so he was suspended at once from his teaching post.'

'Suspended at once?' Holly asked in a horrified voice. 'Without even a hearing?' She was astounded at her own quick leap to his defence.

'Not at all. The suspension was only temporary, pending a formal hearing by the academic senate.'

'Then the hearing must have vindicated him,' Holly returned stoutly, remembering all too well the lengths to which he'd gone to avoid compromising circumstances on the field trip—even if those efforts had backfired so ludicrously.

Dr Kirkland shook her head sadly. 'It did—completely—but he resigned before it was held. He simply refused to fight the charge. I'm afraid he was too hot-headed to listen, and too proud—

some people said too arrogant—to defend himself before the senate.'

This was information that didn't surprise Holly in the least. 'You mean he just quit? He didn't have to leave?'

'Exactly. He stormed into the chancellor's office, as I understand it, and told him that if the university had no more faith in him than it was showing at the moment, he had no wish to be a part of it. And that was that. As far as he was concerned, the academic community hadn't measured up. He turned his back on it, and moved out here to open his own Institute near Sequim.'

Holly bristled with indignation for him. 'Well, good for Dr Alexander! He's certainly shown them all,' she said, wondering at the fervent loyalty which she'd had no idea she possessed. 'There isn't a more brilliant botanist in the United States. He can run rings around any university professor in the country. Why, they're all years behind him——' Suddenly remembering to whom she was talking, she stopped, embarrassed. 'I mean——'

'No need to apologise.' Dr Kirkland laughed. 'I agree with you.' Then she sobered, a gentle frown furrowing her forehead. 'But what a loss it's been! His laboratory here on the peninsula is excellent, but even with all the wealth he's poured into it, it's small compared to the giant university labs. Just imagine what he could have accomplished if he'd had the resources of a Stanford or a Harvard at his disposal. But after six years he's still a renegade, still doing it on his own rather than co-operating with the academic establishment.'

And he's still avoiding idiotic schoolgirls like the plague, Holly thought ruefully, hearing an echo of his sardonic voice. She sighed and settled back into her chair. 'Well, it certainly helps explain why he didn't want anything to do with another female student,' she said shrugging. 'And in light of that, *and* that disastrous field trip, I'd have no chance at all.'

'Indeed you would. Remember, you'll graduate in June; you won't be a student any more. With your BA in hand, as far as he's concerned you'll just be another botanist receiving on-the-job training. Besides, by now he's probably realised he over-reacted to your little misdeeds on the field trip. At least you can apply and give it a chance, can't you?' Dr Kirkland urged. 'What have you got to lose?'

My pride and dignity, for two things, reflected Holly glumly, but she promised to think about it. Her thoughts were in confusion as she emerged from the office, application form held irresolutely in one hand. Her professor's revelation about Jon Alexander's past—as sketchy and tantalising as it was—had helped, in a way. She could feel the bitter resentment she'd carried with her for six months ebbing away. But she certainly had no desire to go through the embarrassment of facing him again—she wasn't sure in fact, if she could. But on the other hand, Dr Kirkland was right, she really was.

What in the world was she going to do?

Holly had planned on spending a few hours in the school's research library before driving to Lake

Quinault for the weekend, but she knew she didn't have a ghost of a chance of concentrating—on anything—until she'd made up her mind one way or the other. With things the way they were, she might as well head off to Lake Quinault early. Perhaps Clint and Mary could help her decide.

Mary, clasping her knitting needles and trailed by a ball of yellow wool bumping erratically behind her, greeted Holly with a hug.

'What are you doing here? I thought you were going to be at the library this afternoon.'

'I couldn't concentrate.' Holly reached down and retrieved the unravelling, fluffy wool. 'I didn't know you could knit.'

'I can't,' Mary said, with a laugh, 'but I thought I'd give it a try for the baby's sake.' She held aloft a needle from which dangled a snarled scrap of yellow. 'Guess what it's going to be.'

'A blanket?' Holly said doubtfully. 'A hat?'

'Really!' Mary said. 'It'll be a bootie. At least it's supposed to be, but did you know knitting instructions are all for right-handed people? Or at least the ones I have are, so I'm having a terrible time!'

Smiling, Holly curled up in one of the easy chairs close to the gentle, dry warmth of the old-fashioned Franklin stove while her sister-in-law settled across from her. 'How *is* the baby?' Holly asked. The news of Mary's pregnancy had provided the only bright spot in Holly's life during the gloomy months since last September.

'He's kicking,' Mary replied proudly, resting her

hand on her swelling abdomen. 'Now, what's this about not being able to concentrate?'

Holly sighed deeply. 'Dr Kirkland's trying to talk me into applying for that internship after all, and I just don't know what to do.'

'Well, I don't think you should have anything to do with Jon Alexander or his Institute,' Mary responded firmly. 'You haven't been yourself since that field trip, and to tell you the truth Clint and I have been getting worried about you.'

'I'm sorry,' Holly said guiltily. And here she thought she'd been so clever about covering up her depression when she was with them. 'I didn't mean to give you two anything to worry about. I thought I'd been super-cheerful.'

'You were, dear,' Mary said soothingly. 'That's what gave you away. Don't you worry about getting the money to get through your post-graduate studies. There are loans, you know, and you can keep working part time. And Clint and I can help.'

The kitchen door banged and Clint's big frame came through the doorway. 'Clint and I can help with what?' he asked, tweaking Holly's ponytail affectionately on his way to kiss Mary on the cheek. 'And why aren't you at the library, sis? I thought you had some work to do.'

'She can't concentrate,' Mary answered for her. 'It's that internship. She's thinking about applying.'

Clint's face turned grim. 'Don't do it, Holly. I don't want you having anything to do with that character. Mary's right; we'll get you through somehow.'

As her brother echoed Mary's words, Holly realised with a surge of affection that they'd talked this over before, and they really were ready to help. Her eyes flickered around the room. It was bright and cosy and comfortable, but most of the furniture was second-hand and Holly knew—not that they'd ever say so—that they went without luxuries to help her pay her tuition. How much they'd already given her! Not only financially, but emotionally too. No, she couldn't let them do any more, even if they wanted to, not with a baby on the way.

Even without the baby, it was time she started standing on her own two feet, taking care of herself—and making her own decisions. And clearly, the intelligent decision in this case was to swallow her pride and go for the internship. If she was turned down (which, of course, she would be, despite Dr Kirkland's assurances) at least she would have given it a try.

Three weeks later, Holly unfolded a sheet of paper left in her dormitory mailbox to find a brief command: See me re: application. A. A. Kirkland.

So the great Dr Jon Alexander had already made his decision and informed Dr Kirkland, who was her sponsor. Somehow it annoyed her that he had been so prompt. She steeled herself as she trotted down the flight of stone steps to the lower level of the green campus, where Dr Kirkland's office in the Life Sciences building was located. She would not be disappointed. She had never really wanted to apply in the first place, she had done so only at her professor's urging, and she had never believed she had a chance. Rejection, therefore, would come as no surprise, so what was there to be disappointed about? Nevertheless, her stomach was knotted tight with an anxious, resentful depression. As nice as it was of Dr Kirkland to want to break the news to her in person, she wished her professor had simply put it in the impersonal note in her mailbox. Holly stopped outside the office door. With eyes closed, she took a deep breath, then turned the door knob and walked gamely in.

Dr Kirkland, whose smile was rare and usually somewhat stiff, was grinning broadly. She was also waving a letter. 'It's yours! You've got it!'

Holly had read about hearts skipping beats but this was the first time it had actually happened to her. And her heart wasn't the only thing that was acting peculiarly. A series of long, slow shivers ran caterpillar-like down her spine, from neck to waist, her stomach seemed to be somewhere down around her knees, and her knees themselves felt as if they weren't there at all.

The only time she had felt anything remotely like it was the first time she'd been on a roller-coaster, when she was eight years old. She had laughed with pleasure all the way up the long incline, as the car jigged and creaked its slow way to the summit. And then at the very top the car had stopped momentarily, seemingly in the sky, poised precariously over the awesome, near-vertical descent it was about to make. The laughter had died when she peeped over the edge, and she had felt—well, about the way she felt now.

Maybe the similarity was no accident. Maybe she was poised on a different kind of summit with the prospect of an even more frightening plunge before her. For she knew it was not the excitement of her success, or the challenge of the internship that had paralysed her there in the doorway of Room 206, it was the knowledge that she would once again be meeting Jon Alexander. She'd be face to face with the man who, in just three short days, months and months ago, had turned her steady, bright world upside down and grey; a man who still appeared in her dreams with surprising, irritating frequency. A billow of panic welled up inside her. She hadn't honestly thought she'd have to go through seeing him again. Could she, when it came down to it?

Misinterpreting Holly's reaction, Dr Kirkland laughed and motioned her to a chair. 'Sit down before you fall down. Believe me, I'm as excited as you are. Isn't it marvellous? Congratulations!'

Holly, trying to pull herself together, smiled weakly.

'Don't look so worried. You're the finest young botanist around, and I know you'll do brilliantly.' Dr Kirkland leaned forward across her desk, her face more sober. 'But I hope you'll accept a little advice: maintain a totally professional demeanour whenever you're in his presence. Keeping your relationship on an entirely impersonal, unemotional basis is the key to getting along with Jon Alexander.'

Oh sure, thought Holly wryly, that's just what I'll do. Nothing to it. Only how do you maintain an impersonal relationship with a man who had spent the night in a sleeping bag with you the last time you'd met—and whose last sight of you had been when he'd awakened to find your barely clothed body lying beneath him?

CHAPTER FIVE

The Alexander Institute.
No Admittance Without Prior Authorisation.
At the sight of the sign over the entrance gate,
Holly's insides churned and quivered, and her foot
leapt involuntarily against the car's accelerator.
The aged and battered Ford jumped forward, then
sputtered and died only a few yards inside the
gate.

'Oh, damn!' Holly muttered, switching off the
ignition key. 'I can't be late . . . I just can't.'

She gave the car a moment's respite, then
gingerly turned on the key and pressed the
accelerator. The engine coughed hopefully, but
then clanked and was quiet. She pumped on the
pedal, gnawing nervously at her lower lip, praying
it would start before she flooded the carburettor.
And it did.

'Thank God.' Weakly, she sank back against the
seat, feeling the sweet relief flow through her.
Nursing the car along with all the care she knew
how to give it, she continued down the long drive
that wound through the Institute's grounds.
Stalling the car, she knew, hadn't been an accident
but a result of the agitation she'd been living with
since learning the news in April. With intelligent,
adult determination, she'd been schooling herself
to think of Jon Alexander not as a person, but as a

77

temporary employer, no more. A rueful smile played about her lips. Sure. And then at the mere sight of his name, she practically gets hysterical. It was a warning of just how difficult things were going to be, despite her mental preparations. If she didn't keep a firm, controlling hand on her emotions, her future was likely to be a mess.

Her future. Holly glanced at her watch. Incredibly, it was three forty-five p.m. on 5 June, and the future was the present. Her entrance interview and orientation tour was just minutes away.

The first view of the Institute building itself was more than a bit intimidating—and the closer she came, the more intimidating it got. It was bigger than she expected, and more modern, with a kind of flashy simplicity; a long, low-slung building of glass and steel nestled in the thick trees of a green, sloping sward. She couldn't see Sequim Bay from the road, but she knew the mouth of it lay just beyond the sward, right below the building. What a location! Private, too. The several acres of meadow and forest she'd driven through were more than enough to ensure that.

Holly glanced down at her clothes for reassurance. To celebrate her success in getting the internship she'd splurged on a new suit and a few other nice things, and now she was very glad she had. Yes, they looked fine. The eggshell-blue silk blouse and well-tailored grey linen suit looked as good on her as it had in the shop. The accessories—low-heeled grey pumps, handbag, and small silver hoop earrings—were appropriately conservative. Inspecting herself in the rear-view mirror, she was relieved to see that her long black hair, gleaming with blue highlights, was still pulled smoothly into a chignon and anchored securely with pins. There was no question but that she looked like a professional, competent and business-like, and very different from the Holly of last September.

Why, then, couldn't she make herself feel more confident? Why was her smooth skin flushed, her mouth dry with nervousness, her fingers a little tremulous? Well, never mind. She was simply not going to let herself turn this summer into a re-run of that disastrous fieldtrip; absolutely not. And no matter how she felt inside, she would die before she'd give the slightest inkling of her inner turmoil to That Man.

That Man—whose curious physical effect on her was as potent as ever, if not more so—was clearly intent on rattling her, and he wasn't even making an effort to hide it. At least he'd waited until his secretary, after escorting her into his quiet, spacious and surprisingly luxurious office, had retreated and closed the door behind her.

'I'm surprised you had the courage to apply,' Jon Alexander said indolently, tossing down his silver fountain pen, leaning back against a high-backed, leather swivel chair, and eyeing her across the rich oak expanse of an oversized desk.

'I don't know why you should be,' Holly retorted coolly, meeting his penetrating eyes and doing her best to give him the wide-eyed, innocent stare she'd perfected in front of her dormitory mirror. 'It's only natural that I'd try for a position like this. Besides, my sponsor, Dr Kirkland, wanted me to apply.' Otherwise, God knows, she wouldn't have dreamed of darkening his door-step—not in a million years, not after what had happened.

That wide-eyed stare had been a lot easier to put on in front of a mirror, and it must have been a flop, because he seemed to look right into her mind. She forced herself not to blink or look away while those vivid, lucid green eyes seemed to scorch her face with their cold fire.

'I see,' he said, his voice a calm, icy drawl. 'Your career's so important to you that you're willing to swallow that charming little parting speech of yours.'

Why couldn't he let the past alone? Was this the way it was going to be from now on? Had she worked so hard to subdue her whirling emotions, her bitter resentment, only for him to badger her in that cruel, careless way the first chance he got? Anger flooded through her in a hot, surging tide, but that too she controlled. It was anger, all right, not nervousness or mortification, and the thought reassured her.

'You're referring, I suppose, to my remark about never wanting to see you again,' Holly replied evenly, tilting her chin upwards. 'It was childish of me, I admit. But considering the circumstances, I'd hardly think that someone of your stature would hold it against me, Dr Alexander.'

Although he didn't seem the slightest bit nonplussed by her counter-attack, Holly drew courage from the unemotional, self-possessed way she'd managed to deliver it. Actually, now that she was finally face to face with him, it wasn't nearly as terrifying as she'd feared, even if he was doing his best to be disagreeable. A part of her confidence came from her appearance—she looked like a different person even if she didn't quite feel like one. Important, too, was an awareness that she was meeting him on a far more equal footing, since she was now a *bona fide* botanist herself—a fledgeling, true, but a botanist none the less. And most important was her earnest, steely determination not to let him reduce her again to that fumbling, brainless state of idiocy. Not ever.

Again he seemed to read her thoughts. His mouth curled sardonically, and his dangerous green eyes insolently and openly raked her from chignon to sleek grey pumps. Under that scorching gaze Holly's spunky self-assurance hesitated, sputtered, and died, as miserably as her car's engine had a few minutes before. It took every ounce of her remaining courage not to leap from her chair and run. But she didn't run, and when he finally lifted his eyes to hers, she met them steadily, though now her heart was hammering wildly and her mouth was as dry as cotton wool. From the brazen way he'd examined her, she knew he'd taken in her new exterior, then mentally stripped her as bare as she'd been the last time he'd seen her—and then some, probably.

'No,' he said at last, 'I have no intention of

holding it against you.' Then, surprisingly, 'And as you'll soon find out, we're a rather informal, close-knit group, so let's dispense with the "Dr Alexander". Besides,' he added, his voice laced with sarcasm, as his eyes flicked over her once more, 'don't you think formality's a little silly between people who've slept together?'

She choked back the gasp that rose naturally. 'Yes, I suppose it would be, at that,' she managed to reply steadily, although for a moment there she had considered hitting him with the heavy ceramic ashtray perched on the corner of his desk. She did allow herself a stab of defiance by adding a 'Jon' that was as pert and impudent as she could make it.

Whether or not she was fooling him she couldn't tell, but she wasn't fooling herself. The self-possession, such as it was, about which she'd been so proud only a few moments ago, was no more than skin-deep. Underneath, her emotions were fluctuating like seismograph needles in the middle of an earthquake. Knowing the way her eyes mirrored her feelings, she lowered her glance, trying frantically to compose her whirling thoughts. Never in her wildest imagination had she thought he'd refer to that night. And the *way* he'd done it—so casually—and he'd made it sound like they'd ... they'd ... How could he? How did he dare ...! But then, she reminded herself belatedly, she'd never dreamed he'd hire her, either.

He had, though, and that was worth some thinking about. She'd been so busy worrying about how *she* felt, and her own motivation for applying that she'd given little thought to his reasons for choosing her. Could it be that he, too, wasn't able to get that weekend out of his mind? And was that why he was giving her so difficult a time? No, that was completely ridiculous. There was no point in letting her imagination run away with itself. He'd probably felt forced—out of an ingrained sense of fair play—to give her the internship, since she was the most qualified candidate. Obviously he really hadn't wanted to, and so he was determined to extract his pound of flesh in retaliation. Or perhaps this personal and highly suggestive conversation was a simple ploy on his part to embarrass her into quitting. Then he'd feel free to appoint another candidate. If so, he could think again.

The sound of his straightening somewhat impatiently in his chair ended her reflections. After taking a steadying breath, she looked up. To her surprise, his expression was as businesslike as a bank teller's, and he was examining a large, flat book bound in maroon leather, his appointment calendar. Relief flooded through her. Either he'd given up trying to bait her or he'd run out of time. Now he had to get back to his own affairs, thank goodness, and pass her on to the person with whom she'd be working this summer. The worst had to be over.

'I've asked my secretary to help you find a place to rent,' he said, still studying the calendar.

'That won't be necessary. One of my old botany professors has a house near here, but she's in Europe this summer. She's given me her house to use, in exchange for my looking after her Airedales.'

Jon's thick, russet eyebrows lifted. 'Would that be Dr Kirkland on West Sequim Bay Road?'

'Y-yes.'

'Well, well,' he said, and her heart quailed as she saw him fight back a smile. 'We're practically neighbours, then,' he closed the appointment calendar and slapped it down on the desk, and now he did smile, but it was thin, probing, unreadable '. . . in addition to working together.'

'Working together,' she repeated dully, her mind whirling once again. Practically neighbours! That meant he lived in one of those exclusive-looking homes on the rise above Dr Kirkland's house. That was bad enough, but compared to 'working together'—if that was really what he meant—it was a minor complication. Anxiety swept over her in slow, rolling waves. 'But won't I be working with one of your staff members?' She bit her lower lip to keep it from trembling. 'I mean, I was led to understand that the intern doesn't work directly under you.'

'Ordinarily, you'd be right,' he said off-handedly, but she was sure he could see the canyon-like cracks rapidly splintering her composure. His eyes gleamed with amusement, and his smile, no longer unreadable, was sardonic and taunting. 'However, my research has taken me more and more into mycology . . . your speciality. So, after a couple of days of training, which you'll do under my senior lab technician, Lillian Helmut, you'll be working with me. Closely.'

It seemed to Holly that he'd put a measured, deliberate emphasis on the last word and then calmly watched her to see what the reaction would be. Holly matched his stare and willed her face into wooden immobility, but—damn him!—she felt the familiar warm flush move up to her throat and rise visibly to her cheeks.

It seemed to satisfy him. He consulted his watch and rose. 'I've just enough time to give you a brief tour of the main building and to introduce you to some of the staff.' Blandly, he added, 'Standard treatment for new personnel.'

Unable to order her jumbled thoughts, the following half-hour passed in a blur for her, with only a few distinct impressions. One was that the Institute laboratories were the kind of immaculate and ultra-modern workplaces you saw in movies about the twenty-first century. Another was the serene sense of teamwork that pervaded the place: the staff of capable, dedicated professionals respected each other and themselves—and obviously worshipped the ground Jon Alexander walked on. She could see it in their eyes, their manner, the way they spoke to him—a simple respect and admiration that enveloped him like a cloud wherever he went. And a liking, too—which frankly surprised her even in her muddled and distracted state. Because as devastatingly attractive as he was, he most certainly didn't rank high on her list of the world's most likeable men.

When Jon finally led her back past the administrative office and to the reception area, Holly at last managed to pull herself together. It was suddenly shatteringly clear that she couldn't go through with it. If it wasn't possible to put together a coherent thought in his physical presence (whether it was or wasn't a plot on his part was immaterial), then how could she work closely with him? Despite all the resolve in the world she might as well quit and be done with it. And now was the time to do it. But before she could get any words out, Jon swivelled his tall, lean frame round towards her.

'I'll expect you tomorrow at eight sharp.' He pushed open the door for her. 'And don't even think about quitting.' His rugged, sardonic face moved closer, lit by the ghost of a smile in his eyes. 'So stop rehearsing your resignation speech.'

Thoroughly floored, Holly flushed crossly. Could he read everyone's mind, or just hers? And if he hadn't been trying to make her quit then why had he worked so hard to embarrass her by dragging up that night in the tent?

'I don't know what you mean,' she prevaricated in self-defence. 'I wouldn't dream of quitting ... no matter how annoying some aspects of the work might be.'

The skin at the sides of his eyes crinkled with humour, but he said nothing, only looked down at her with those clear, green eyes.

Calling on her last ounce of willpower, Holly added coolly, 'I'll see you at eight tomorrow, then. Goodbye.'

She could have sworn she heard a quiet chuckle as she escaped across the planted atrium that served as an entry, so it was with some very murderous and not in the least ladylike thoughts that Holly stalked to her car. She glanced at her wrist-watch after starting the engine—no trouble this time—and was relieved to see that it was after the time Angela Kirkland had said she was leaving for the airport. Never had Holly so desperately needed to be alone, to unwind, to banish all thoughts from her mind and relax. If she didn't, she was sure she'd explode into a million pieces.

And what a perfect place to unwind in, she sighed a few minutes later when she turned down a short, wooded drive to the contemporary A-frame house overlooking Sequim Bay. The sound of her car pulling into the carport set off a cacophany of frantic barking from the dog-run at the side of the house. Well, it was people she wanted to get away from; dogs were another matter. Welcoming their distraction she had to smile. Nothing about Angela Kirkland's living environment had surprised Holly with the exception of the two young Airedales. It wasn't their existence she had found so fascinating earlier that morning when she'd spent a couple of hours with her ex-professor to familiarise herself with the house and the dogs, but their astonishing lack of discipline. Clearly had managed to bamboozle their redoubtable mistress completely—something no student in the history of Port Angeles College had ever been able to do.

'Quiet, Topper. Quiet, Tandy,' Holly scolded in mock sternness as she reached over the fence of the run and calmed the frisky, tan-coloured dogs with a few affectionate pats. 'If you give me five minutes to change my clothes, I'll take you for a run on the beach.'

The tide was out, exposing a narrow strip of kelp-flecked, dark sand, and Holly revelled in the sense of freedom from thought as she ran, her hair streaming behind her, the air salty on her lips. The Airedales capered at her heels as if she were a trusted old friend, until she tired and sank on to the warm sand, savouring the mild evening sunshine. She unleashed the dogs and let them tumble around her unrestricted.

Seeing that they made no attempt to run away, she settled back full length with a sigh, inhaling the sharp fragrance of the sea. She closed her eyes, better to hear the soft sounds of the water lapping rhythmically on the beach, the swoosh of the small gentle waves breaking, the wheeling terns and gulls squabbling over their catches. Behind her, on the low rise, she could hear the breeze ruffling the needles of the thick plantation of Douglas fir.

It was lovely, drowsy, and dreamy, and soothing—for all of three minutes. And then, as if pouring uninvited into the blessedly vacant spaces in her mind, came images of Jon, questions about Jon, doubts, fears ... No, she vowed crossly, pushing them back and sitting up abruptly. She wouldn't think about him yet. Not him, and not his puzzling, maddening behaviour. Not until she'd relaxed enough to deal clearly and unemotionally with her thoughts—and her feelings. But she needed more than good intentions to keep him out of her mind, and she cast rapidly about for an activity. Listening to the wind in the trees certainly wasn't going to do it. Her eyes fell on the dogs.

'I think it's about time you two were trained,' she said, brushing sand out of her long hair and getting to her feet. 'I learned all about animal psychology in Psych 128, and now's the time to apply it. You're going to learn to sit on command.'

Tandy, licking Holly's ankle, looked more amenable to instruction than Topper, who was busy intimidating a tiny hermit crab on a nearby driftwood log, so Holly elected to start with her. 'You first.'

A hilarious hour later, she called it quits. Tandy and Topper could have given a donkey instructions on sheer, joyful stubbornness. Fastening their leashes, she headed homewards, feeling immensely refreshed. Who cared if they wouldn't sit? Just realising that every night after work she could have a relaxing run on the beach with them, followed by a quiet, uneventful evening alone in these beautiful, wooded surroundings made her feel more capable of finishing the summer ahead with her emotional faculties intact.

As her eyes drifted up to the houses further up on the sward, Jon invaded her thoughts again. Why in the world did he derive such perverse pleasure from badgering her? And could she possibly stand a whole summer of it? Never mind a whole summer, could she take even another day? But really, wasn't it only logical to assume today was an exception? After all, he was bound to be engrossed in his experiments throughout the working day; how much time could he possibly have to create havoc with her? And as for his living in one of those houses ahead, what did it matter? She bet he didn't leave the Institute until ten p.m. He just wasn't the kind of man who stopped working at traditional hours.

All very reassuring, even if she wasn't really a hundred per cent self-convinced. Still, she reflected, locking the dogs into the dog-run and returning to the house, at least she didn't have to cope with him again until tomorrow. But it was only ten minutes later, while she was in the middle of unpacking her suitcases, when the doorbell rang that Holly discovered just how wrong her assumptions about the future could be.

'Oh!' she exclaimed aghast, as she opened the oak door to discover Jon Alexander casually but firmly planted on her doorstep.

He smiled wickedly and raised one dark russet eyebrow as he took in the wind-ruffled dark hair cascading around her shoulders and down her back, her brief and frayed cut-off jeans, and her yellow cotton top with its ends knotted together to reveal a bare abdomen.

'Well,' he drawled, as his eyes lingered for a long, bold moment on the sensuous lines of her figure, 'I'm glad to see that the intimidatingly cool and professional-looking Holly Fraser is an office-hours phenomenon.'

'What are you doing here?' she snapped shakily, resisting an impulse to wrap her arms about herself and cover up that mortifyingly naked midriff.

Jon looked unconvincingly aggrieved. 'Being

neighbourly,' he said, gesturing to the large brown paper bag in his hand. 'I assumed you might not have enough time to shop for groceries, so I brought you over some dinner. Speaking of neighbourliness, aren't you going to invite me in?'

Invite him in? Holly's blue eyes widened in amazement. At a loss for speech, she stepped back dazedly and in he walked. Feeling very much like a rabbit who had been tricked into ushering a fox into her burrow she trailed him warily into the living-room.

'Nice,' he said appreciatively, turning in a slow circle to take in the open-beamed ceiling, the oak-railed sleeping loft, the massive rock fireplace, the thick teal-blue carpet, and the comfortable, modern furniture.

The realisation that he was seeing the inside of the house for the first time jolted Holly out of her tongue-tied state. If he was such a neighbourly man, why hadn't he ever visited Dr Kirkland?

'This is certainly generous of you,' Holly said, her words generously laced with sarcasm, as she watched him set the bag down on the counter that divided the kitchen from the living-dining-room. 'But it's completely unnecessary,' she added with a distinct tremor in her voice as she watched him produce a bottle of excellent Chablis from the bag. The thought of an intimate dinner, complete with fine wine, sent the now familiar jelly-like sensations to her knees. Would she spill it on him again?

'I'll stick this into the freezer compartment to cool while we make the sandwiches,' he said smoothly, ignoring her comment.

'Sandwiches!' Holly exclaimed, aware of an absurd—and dangerous—tugging at her heart strings. 'Is that all you usually eat after working all day?'

'Actually, it is,' he answered with a shrug. 'I'm too busy to learn to cook, I get tired of restaurant food after a day or two, and I value my privacy too much to hire live-in help.' He unpacked two ripe avocados, a small jar of mayonnaise, a generous package of fresh Dungeness crabmeat, and a loaf of french bread. Then he looked up at her and grinned engagingly, destroying what little resolve she'd worked up to throw him out. 'But even if I do say so myself, I have sandwiches down to a fine art.'

'I can see that,' Holly ruefully admitted, watching him work competently with all those mouth-watering ingredients. Then realising that he'd sent her off on a tangent and away from the important issue (which was: *Just what was he doing here?*), she dug her heels in and levelled what she hoped was a no-nonsense gaze.

'May I ask, by the way, why this sudden and complete about-face from your usual . . . usual . . .' Holly searched frantically for a diplomatic way to put it.

'. . . usually rude, overbearing, despicable self,' Jon supplied conversationally, as he started slicing the bread. 'I believe those were the words you used last September.'

Holly gritted her teeth. He had the memory of an elephant. 'Exactly.'

He stopped working and leaned casually against

the ceramic-tiled counter. 'It's the only sensible course for me to take if we're going to work well together this summer.' He folded his arms. 'All right, I admit I was angry with you for having the gall to apply for my internship,' he grumbled drily. 'Especially when I realised that I had no choice but to appoint you, since your qualifications were so much better than the other candidates'. And I also admit that maybe I was trying to egg you into leaving.' He shrugged. 'But that was only at first. For some totally irrational reason ... for which I probably should have my head examined ... I changed my mind about your suitability during the tour. Maybe I've been looking at things the wrong way. Anyway, here I am, with a peace offering to a colleague.'

His last word, said quite ungrudgingly, and without the over-emphasis that would have marked it for sarcasm, completely punctured Holly's ballooning anger over his intolerable arrogance. Colleague ... the word sent a warm, bright glow spreading though her, and yet at the same time there was a fresh surge of irritation. It just wasn't fair that all he had to do was throw her one civil word, like a bone to a dog, and there she was, as ready to melt as a bowl of strawberry jelly in a hot oven!

Jon cocked an ear. 'Are those Dr Kirkland's dogs making all that racket?'

'What ...? Yes ... I suppose so. Dr Kirkland only feeds them once a day, about this time. They're probably hungry.'

A smile tugged at the corners of his mouth, and

his green eyes sparkled at the indecision and confusion plastered on her face. 'Well, then,' he said quietly, 'don't you think you ought to feed them?'

Feeling out-manoeuvred and slow-thinking, as she usually seemed to be with him, Holly found herself ruefully following his suggestion. But he was right about calling a truce, she thought, as she went out of the side door and opened the gate of the dog-run.

'Topper! Tandy!'

She didn't have any time for further reflection because the dogs bounded in, almost bowling her over, and made a frantic beeline for the kitchen. Obviously, that was where they were fed.

'Sit,' came an authoritative voice.

Holly rounded the counter in time to see two abashed Airedales skitter to a stop on the tile floor and promptly, if clumsily, obey the instruction. There they sat, tongues lolling, eyes bright with eagerness to follow his next command.

This was too much! In an hour of coaxing she hadn't been able to get one of them to sit down for more than five seconds. Jon hadn't even raised his voice and he had them both in the palm of his hand. Oh, the nerve of him! He was doing it just to irritate her.

'Good dogs,' he said warmly, scratching each behind an ear. Visible adoration leapt into their melting, brown eyes. 'What are their names?'

'Topper and Tandy,' she replied, then muttered, 'alias Traitor and Traitress, the little rats!'

'What did you say?' he asked pleasantly.

'Nothing, nothing at all. I'll get their food.'

She poured dog food into two metal bowls, each with a T on it, which told Holly nothing, and appeared to confuse the dogs as well, because they scuffled energetically over the bowls until Jon looked up from the sandwiches.

'Topper,' he said, and pointed at the right-hand bowl. Topper went quietly. 'Tandy.' His forefinger was levelled at the bowl on the left, to which a somewhat chastened Tandy moved after a brief moment's indecision, and both dogs ate peaceably from their separate bowls.

Then, while he finished making the sandwiches with efficiency and dispatch—the way he did everything, she was sure—Holly filled two bowls with water for them. 'If,' she warned him mentally, 'they fight over this water, and you straighten them out with a single movement of that imperious forefinger, so help me, Jon Alexander, I will dump both bowls over your head.'

Fortunately, that wasn't necessary.

'Shall I light a fire?' he asked, watching her set the table. Holly's back was to him, but she could quite literally feel his eyes running over her uncovered midriff and then down the long length of her shapely bare legs, so that first the skin at her waist tingled, and then the tender, delicate flesh behind her knees. 'Otherwise you'll freeze in that skimpy outfit of yours. The fog's coming in.'

Ever since Jon had walked in the door Holly had been fighting the impulse to run and change; not for warmth, of course, but for protection against those roving, disturbing eyes of his. But if she had, it would have been the same as telling him in so many words that his unexpected presence had altogether unnerved her—which, true as it was, was none of his business.

Strange, she had assumed somehow that, when and if their mutual animosity dampened, the troubling spell she was under would evaporate, too. But it wasn't like that at all, quite the opposite. With no simmering anger clouding the air between them, she was infinitely more aware of how his low-timbred voice quickened the blood in her veins, how every time those cool-hot, grey-green eyes roamed over her, her heart practically stopped. Her only recourse was to bluff.

'A fire would be nice,' she managed to say off-handedly. Then hoping to show him how totally unaffected she was, she added with forced nonchalance, 'Let's light the candles, too. It's pleasant to eat by candlelight, and I get to so rarely.'

'I find that hard to believe,' he said, glancing over his shoulder while he knelt to arrange three or four logs in the fireplace. 'With your looks you must have a dozen boyfriends in the background more than willing to feed you by candlelight.'

'Not really,' she countered, ridiculously pleased by this unintended and far from enthusiastic compliment. 'I've been too busy with college and working to date much. But,' she added matter-of-factly, 'now that I have more time I intend to widen my horizons and get out more.'

'I hope you don't expect to find much exciting night life around Sequim,' he said with a quiet laugh, striking a match and lighting the fire. He straightened and raked his eyes over her face. 'Do you have anyone specifically in mind?'

Holly kept her eyes averted. 'No, but I'm sure there must be a few unattached men in the area for me to meet this summer. Aren't there any at the Institute?' she asked, arranging the gold candles on the table, then bringing the loaded plates of food.

Jon's tone was abrupt. 'Only one: Paul Keller, my marine biologist—and he's completely unsuitable for you.'

'Oh? How so?'

'For one thing Paul's a confirmed bachelor, and for another he's way out of your class,' he replied somewhat stuffily. 'I suppose you might find him attractive, but I suggest—strongly—that you forget about him.'

Holly brushed back the heavy curtain of hair that had fallen forward and tucked it behind her ear. 'You sound more like a big brother than a boss,' she said mockingly. 'I assure you I'm perfectly capable of taking care of myself.' She ignored his sceptically raised eyebrow and decided she had played with fire long enough. It was definitely time for a change of subject.

'If you don't mind talking shop on your time off, I'd love to hear something about your current research.'

To her relief, Jon acquiesced readily. After he poured the wine, they sat down and dug into the heavenly sandwiches, and then between bites he started filling her in on the direction his work was taking.

'If you've been following the news you'll know that the cost of fertiliser has sky-rocketed because most of it is made from oil or natural gas products.' Jon sipped his wine. 'And the underdeveloped countries—at least the ones that don't produce their own oil—are being hit the hardest. You see, they're also the ones with the exploding populations, so they need an ever-increasing supply of food or else they starve—but they can't afford the expensive fertiliser it takes.' He glanced at her to see if she followed him.

In reply Holly nodded. 'And you're working to develop plant strains with naturally greater yields?'

Jon shook his head. 'Genetic modification of plants is the way most research is going, but it's long, slow, and chancy. No, I'm working on a shortcut—a way to help plants get more of their own nutrition from the soil around them ... without any increase in fertiliser.'

At first Holly could barely concentrate, unable to dismiss that ever-present, intrusive awareness of his physical closeness. But he was talking about botany, after all, and if the rather pedantic Angela Kirkland could hold her attention, then certainly Jon Alexander could, with his enthusiasm that was laced so powerfully with brilliance and authority. Soon she was listening intently, all her attention focused on his words.

'. . . you see,' he was saying, leaning forward, the remaining half of his sandwich forgotten, 'there are certain organisms, members of the mushroom family, that you can find in almost every soil. Well, they're generally dormant, but they could be used to help plants do better——'

'The mycorrhizal strains,' she interrupted, as caught up as he was. 'They could increase intake of water and phosphates, especially in non-leguminous plants . . .'

He stared at her, openly impressed, and she glowed. Not for the usual reasons this time, but because she was actually engrossed in animated, technical conversation with Dr Jon Alexander—an adult, fruitful discussion, and she had impressed him. She, Holly Fraser . . .'!

'You know,' he said, 'your grasp of mycology is quite impressive. What got you interested in it in the first place?'

'It was the mushrooms,' she answered, flattered by the real interest in his voice. 'Even as a child I was fascinated by how they'd suddenly appear like magic over night. When I first started to collect them I was just mimicking my brother. I didn't have any playmates who lived nearby and Clint— he's eight years older than I am—certainly wasn't going to play games with me. But he let me tag along sometimes when he went on short hikes. He loves collecting things, especially rocks and insects—I picked mushrooms. When I got a little older he taught me how to mount and preserve them . . .' She smiled. '. . . out of self-defence, probably—my finds tended to stink the house out.'

Jon chuckled. It was an unexpectedly melodious sound that Holly found very attractive. But then what didn't she find attractive about him?

'Anyway,' she continued, 'by the time I left school I'd already decided I was going to be a botanist, so I started to study more systematically, and got interested in the species a lot less magical than mushrooms, like the rusts and mildews. Needless to say, I was considered a rather weird kid.'

'Kids with avid interests usually are,' Jon commiserated. 'I know *I* was.'

It didn't occur to her at the time that they were getting on rather well together as people, and not only as scientists, but they were. She did know that she was sorry when they suddenly realised they'd been talking for hours without ever rising from the table, and it was already after eleven o'clock.

'I plan on keeping you very busy this summer, starting first thing in the morning,' Jon said as he stood up, 'but I hadn't meant to keep you up so late talking botany. You know, you're a hell of an easy person to talk to.' Too easy, he reflected warily, and perhaps habit-forming. 'Anyway, I'll give you a hand with these dishes and be off.'

'I'll take care of them,' Holly replied, smiling. 'It's the least I can do since you brought the food. And.' she added mischievously, 'did all the cooking.'

'You don't have to twist my arm to get me to agree to that,' Jon said, as she walked him to the door. But instead of opening it, he put a hand flat on the wall, leaning over her. All thoughts of phosphates and plant productivity disappeared. She was reminded again of how big he was.

'I'm afraid,' he continued levelly, 'dishes aren't my forte. Usually, I just use paper plates.'

'Paper plates and sandwiches,' Holly said, her heart in her mouth. She tried to back away, but the heavy oak door pressed into her shoulder blades. 'Have you ever thought you might need a wife?'

Oh dear, what a thing to say! Two bright pink spots jumped to her cheeks. She was only trying to be . . . All she'd meant was . . .

He slowly arched an eyebrow. 'Was that a proposal?'

'Of course not . . .' she stammered, her cheeks burning with embarrassment. She dropped her eyes miserably to the floor. 'I . . . I only meant . . . oh, you know what I meant.'

Did he? Did *she*?

He placed a finger beneath her chin and tilted her head upward. He smiled broadly, and then his grin turned a little wry. 'You're sweet, Holly, do you know that?'

She started to speak, but he cut her off. 'I know it's not the sort of thing to say to a woman these days, but you *are* sweet. You're——'

Holly, her misery of a moment before turning to euphoria, felt him suddenly check himself. He dropped his hand from her chin.

'To answer your question: yes, I've thought once or twice that it might be nice to have a wife, but frankly, my work comes first. I just don't have time for one. Anyway, the chances are that I'd get stuck with a woman who doesn't like washing dishes any more than I do. And speaking of battles between the sexes,' he said, his voice all at once impatient and authoritative, his piercing eyes riveted to hers, 'I meant what I said about Paul Keller. Don't even think about it. He's big league.'

Now the euphoria vanished too. Resenting his presumptuousness—after all, she hadn't even met this Paul character—and his second attempt at playing a bullying big brother, Holly's cornflower-blue eyes deepened with temper.

'And I'm only little league?' she said sarcastically. 'Thanks, but——'

He didn't give her a chance to finish, but, amazingly, hauled her against him. She was too startled to resist as his mouth fastened on hers. And if she hadn't been so astonished, would she have resisted anyway? The moment his lips touched hers she melted like a wax figurine thrust into a hot flame.

Jon's feelings weren't so very different. He had meant to shock her, to show her with a brutal, ruthless kiss just how inexperienced she was, but the sweet, soft, yielding of her lips drove every rational thought from his head. His eyes closed, and he pressed her still more tightly to him, his tongue exploring her mouth hungrily.

Flames raced and sizzled through Holly's body. Like Jon, she was drowning in the kiss, unsure of whether she was responding, unsure of how much time was passing, unsure even of where she was. Slowly, through a glowing, confused haze, she became aware that his hands were moving compellingly down her back, moulding her to him, forcing her against the long, heated length of him. Her hands slid trembling up his muscular chest, along the smooth skin of his firm, lean neck, and finally came to rest twined in the thick russet hair she'd longed to smooth and caress practically from the first moment she'd seen him. Her fingers tightened in his hair, and she clung to him with a natural, instinctive passion. She was breathless; sensations of pleasure she'd never felt before slithered through her, racing to explode at nerve endings she didn't know she had.

Dazedly, she felt his hands, trailing fire, slide up from her bare waist and slip under her thin blouse to cup the cool softness of her breasts. A shaft of pure, clear ecstasy, so deep and thrilling that she hardly knew if it was pain or joy, shot through her like a bolt of lightning. My God, what was happening? She couldn't let him ... But she couldn't—wouldn't?—draw back. All she could do was stand there powerless, engulfed in her own incredible sensations, wondering whether this was heaven she was in, or hell.

Then, with a harsh and abrupt intake of breath, Jon pulled his lips from hers and dropped his hands from her breasts, their nipples now achingly taut in involuntary invitation.

'I think that ought to make the point,' he ground out. 'Any experienced man could have you in bed in about three minutes.'

Stunned, humiliated, hardly believing he could be that cruel, Holly stood paralysed for a moment, blinking back sudden tears. The arrogance of him, thinking she would have succumbed to him so easily and completely—to any other man, for that matter. Her hand flew up to strike his insolent face, but he caught her wrist easily and forced her straining hand down with no apparent effort.

'What you need is a nursemaid,' he drawled

with sardonic satisfaction. He opened the door behind him and stepped out into the night, then turned to face her again. 'But since there's no one else around to take care of you, I guess I'm elected.'

CHAPTER SIX

IT was far into the small hours of the night, after a hundred futile attempts to stop tossing and turning, and force herself to go to sleep, that Holly finally admitted the truth. She'd tried to run away from it from the moment Jon Alexander had walked into the Quinault Valley Inn's restaurant.

At first she'd told herself it was no more than hero worship, then that it was hero worship with a certain amount of sexual attraction. Then, even before that first evening's comedy of errors was over, she'd admitted that, well, it might be a pretty strong sexual attraction. And after the disastrous field trip, she had tried to convince herself that the alarming current of feeling was hate. But now, after tonight, she knew that those explanations weren't enough; they didn't explain the extraordinary and bewildering welter of conflicting emotions—and responses—that had leapt up in her when he'd taken her in his arms.

No, only one emotion could really explain why she felt so completely alive—and wildly distraught—in his presence, and so half-dead, depressed, and gloomy (for eight months, no less!) in his absence.

She'd fallen in love with Jon Alexander, and she'd done it at first sight.

She stared up at the dimly visible, steeply-pitched ceiling, facing the unbelievable. Love at first sight ... how trite and hackneyed it sounded—until it happened to you. Holly had never even believed the phenomenon really occurred outside books. Indeed, the scientist in her rejected it outright. For all the good it did her.

Bleakly, she examined her plight. She dismissed out of hand the possibility that Jon had fallen in love with her too. With his money, his reputation— and that damned sexiness that radiated from him even when he was talking about phosphates and mushrooms—he could have any woman he wanted. Why would he be interested in her? Besides, the fact that he had made no attempt to contact her during those long months after the field trip made it abundantly clear that there was simply nothing there on his part. Well, not quite nothing, but his own evident awareness of her was obviously strictly physical and only set off by her actual presence. Otherwise, out of sight, out of mind.

So what did all this amount to? The fact that she had darned well better check her out-of-control emotions, or she'd find herself chasing him. A mortifying prospect!

But the knowledge that this very minute he was sleeping just a few doors down (a short, easy walk through the dark, whispering trees) was torture. All she'd have to do was to knock on his door—— She shut her eyes tightly, frowning. For a supposedly intelligent girl, she wasn't being very sensible. That kind of wistful fantasy did nothing but add to her troubles. She needed to use her intellect, not her hormones—or whatever it was that came up with those enticing, pointless daydreams—and work out a rational strategy of self-defence.

Maybe, she thought, grasping for straws, she had simply been ripe to fall in love with any man, and Jon Alexander just happened to be handy. If so, then she could fight fire with fire by meeting other attractive men. She'd start by looking up Paul what's-his-name, whether Jon liked it or not, and if he didn't do the trick, she'd call Anne and ask her to line her up with some dates. Eventually someone would be bound to click, and then that would be that for Jon Alexander.

There, she thought fuzzily, her eyelids finally drifting sleepily down, that's a good, rational approach. Shows what scientific thinking can do. Maybe the logic wasn't exactly foolproof, but ... with a sigh she turned on her side and pulled the covers up to her chin.

She was awake with the first grey, tentative fingers of dawn filtering through the branches beyond the window. The muzzy strategy she'd worked out just before falling asleep no longer seemed as sound as it had, but she quashed her reservations. She had to do something, and until another plan came along, this was it.

A brisk early-morning walk along the beach with the dogs cleared some of the cobwebs from her brain. Then she treated herself to a more substantial breakfast than usual to counteract her nearly sleepless night. Once fortified, and feeling more confident, she showered, dressed, and drove the short distance down West Sequim Bay Road to the Institute, keeping her mind firmly off last night. This was her first day of work, no more, no less—and that was more than enough to think about.

As she got out of her car, a white Buick years past its prime but carefully kept, pulled into the next space. The driver, like her car, was well into middle age and comfortably overweight, but neat and tidy as a button. It was Lillian Helmut, Jon's senior lab technician, who was to train her over the next few days. Since Holly had every intention of sticking leech-like to as many people as possible to minimise the likelihood of finding herself alone with Jon Alexander, she waited for the woman to join her.

'Ready for your first day on the job?' Lillian asked with a ready smile as they walked together up the curving walkway to the entrance.

'Yes, but I'm afraid I'm a little nervous.'

'Just first-day jitters,' Lillian said reassuringly.

If only that was all it was, thought Holly, signing in at the reception desk after the older woman.

They walked through the atrium, past the administrative office alive with the sound of clicking typewriters, and then along the main corridor to the laboratories. Despite her tremors of apprehension about facing Jon in the cold light of day, today at least Holly was capable of taking in her environment fully—an environment that had only been a blur with him at her side. Everything around her bespoke Jon's good taste—

or his ability to choose a decorator. The walls,
ceilings and carpets of the Institute were in muted,
neutral tones of beige, tan and ivory—relaxing and
nice to look at but never distracting. Here and
there along the walls, leafy plants in brightly
coloured pots relieved the coolness, and all the
doors were a surprising, cheerful blue, like jaunty
grace-notes in an atmosphere that might otherwise
have been just a little too sedate.

What a beautiful place to work. How thrilled
and excited she'd be—if not for this complication
she didn't even want to think about—at the
prospect of her first day as a member of Jon
Alexander's research team.

'You'll find that Jon will always be in the
laboratory by the time you arrive,' Lillian said,
with a hint of maternal disapproval in her voice, as
they headed for the botany lab. 'He comes in at
some ungodly hour—six, I think—which means he
typically puts in a fourteen-hour day.' She
frowned. 'Far too much, to my way of thinking,
but Jon Alexander is a law unto himself, as you'll
soon find out.'

Tell me about it, Holly said silently, repressing a
wry grin.

'Anyway,' Lillian continued blithely, 'you'll find
your instructions for the day always written on the
blackboard just inside the door. He'll only expect
you to work from eight to five, of course; he
recognises, even if he doesn't completely approve,
that other people are only human. And do be sure
to take your lunch break, even if he doesn't,' she
added, pausing at the door to the main laboratory.

Taking a deep, steadying breath, Holly followed Lillian into the lab. Her eyes flew to a long, built-in table, fitted with shining, stainless-steel sinks, with rows of shelves overhead and cupboards below. This was the bench—the universal work-place for basic research scientists, and sure enough, Jon was leaning absorbedly over a dissecting microscope. Hearing their footsteps, he straightened absent-mindedly, greeted them with an abstracted but not unfriendly grunt, and returned to work.

Holly wasn't sure what she'd expected, but it certainly wasn't that. Irrationally, she was more than a little piqued. After all, there she had been, in a nerve-racking dither since he'd left her the evening before, and he obviously hadn't bothered to give her a second thought—at least not since he'd arrived at work and his precious microscope!

On the other hand, why get so upset? After all, if he put his personal thoughts aside when he was working, it was going to make the summer a great deal easier. Besides, in the grand scheme of things, his work was infinitely more important than Holly Fraser was, so who was she to get annoyed when he buried himself in it? Thoroughly chastened, she resolved to follow his example and apply herself just as professionally to her own job. Ignoring Jon as much as possible—that is, refusing to let her eyes slide in his direction more than once every ten minutes—she focused all her attention on Lillian.

Surprisingly, the morning passed quickly. For one thing, if Jon ever looked in her direction she never saw it. And for another, Lillian was competently demonstrating a difficult technique Holly needed to know, but had little familiarity with: how to embed fragile, soft, tiny specimens in plastic and then use the hand-cranked microtome to pare paper-thin slices for microscopic analysis.

It was almost lunch-time when the technician took her through the last few steps.

'There. After you put the tissue slice on a glass slide, set it on the slide warmer. The heat makes the plastic adhere. Then,' the woman said, taking her over to a corner work-bench under a hooded vent, 'you stain it.' Lillian tapped the hood. 'Be sure the fan's on so all of the vapours get sucked out. The last step is putting on the transparent slide cover. And that's it,' she concluded, smiling. 'Now it's ready for Jon to examine.'

'Whew,' Holly sighed, 'I hope I followed all that.'

'Don't worry, it just takes practice, and you'll get plenty of that this afternoon.' Lillian glanced at her watch and stretched. 'Time to break. I have some errands to do in Sequim over lunch. You're welcome to ride along if there's anything you need to do in town.'

'No, thanks,' Holly answered, rubbing the back of her neck. She'd been bending over the delicate tissue samples for almost four hours. 'I've brought a packed lunch, and if the fog's lifted I think I'd like to go down to the beach and eat there . . . if there's a way to get down from the sward, that is.'

'Yes, you can drive down the access road.' Lillian paused, eyeing Holly's solidly-heeled pumps with approval. 'But if you want some exercise there are some steps out the back—a hundred and eighty of them.' Her eyes rolled upwards. 'They're not bad going down, but they're murder coming up. While you're down there you ought to peep in and have a look at the marine biology lab if you have time. I know Paul Keller would be glad to show you around, if he's not out at lunch.'

Now *that*, Holly thought with satisfaction, she would most definitely find time to do. It looked like she was going to be able to put her plan to work sooner than she'd thought.

'I'd like to see everything I can,' she said, 'so I'll certainly do that. I wanted to meet Paul Keller anyway.'

She couldn't resist stealing another glance at Jon, and out of the corner of her eye, she saw his head snap up from his microscope. Unable to stop herself she turned, looked straight across the room at him, and caught the full force of his simmering gaze. So he wasn't as totally lost in his work as he'd seemed, she reflected, her eyes defiantly meeting his. It was something to remember.

As Lillian turned to tell him they were leaving for lunch, Holly saw his neutral and disinterested expression return. But, as she managed to escape without any conversation with him by dogging Lillian's heels out of the door, Holly was distinctly aware of two angry, laser-beam eyes burning neat little holes in the middle of her back. Well, fine. Let him glower. She didn't mind in the least giving him something to think about.

The fog had melted away, as it did most mornings, and the day was actually sunny—always an unexpected treat in western Washington. Today was especially beautiful, not a cloud on the horizon. Indeed, it was one of those rare, glorious, clear days when one could see an incredible distance. Before she descended the steps she took a few minutes to savour the sight of the ragged, sawtoothed Cascade mountain range to the east, and towering Mount Baker, glacier-wreathed and magnificent, across the bay further north. Although the thick fir trees blocked the view of the Olympics behind her she knew they were there, cooling the air with the clean winds from their glacial fields, and in the far north the distant horizon was rimmed by Canada's coastal range, all but looming Mount Garibaldi made insignificant by the distance. She was ringed by mountains, except for a narrow gateway—the glittering, twenty-mile-wide Strait of Juan de Fuca, the waterway that linked Puget Sound with the Pacific Ocean. How perfect it all was. As she had many times before, she breathed a sigh of thankfulness that this cool, green Olympic Peninsula, the northwesternmost tip of land in the United States was her home.

She glanced back at the building behind her. That, too, was perfect. Everything about the Institute: the goals, the work environment, the wonderful location ... everything, that is, but its director, with whom she'd never known and never would know a moment's peace. If it weren't for that little difficulty, she would have been content to spend her career here. But as things stood, it was going to take all her ingenuity and control to last the summer.

She walked slowly down the series of steep steps cut into the sward to a cluster of buildings on the edge of Sequim Bay, where a small dock jutted out into the sparkling blue water. Suppressing her normal reserve, Holly tapped tentatively on the opened door of a warehouse-like structure, at the back of which an attractive, brown-haired man of medium height with a full, closely cropped beard was engrossed at a waist-high dissecting table, a scalpel and probe in his hands.

At her knock a friendly smile lit his open features and he beckoned her inside. 'Hi. I'm Paul Keller.'

Frank brown eyes met hers, and to her delight Holly was immediately at ease. It took her a few seconds to figure out who he reminded her of, and surprisingly, it turned out to be Anne. Paul Keller projected the same candid, easy-going amicability that her best friend did. Holly had liked Anne at first sight, and never had cause to change her mind, and she felt the same way about the bearded marine biologist.

'You must be Holly Fraser,' he said, and his eyes lit up as he took a closer look. 'Now I can see why Jon's been keeping you to himself.' He stepped to a stainless-steel sink and carefully washed his hands. 'Formaldehyde,' he explained. 'I've been dissecting a crab.' He came forward to shake hands.

Holly couldn't help being flattered by the lively admiration in his eyes. Unfortunately, however, although she tuned her senses inwards, she didn't feel her pulse accelerate or her throat clog up with nerves as he held her hand a little longer than was strictly necessary. In a way, it was a good thing, because it was clear to her that Paul's charm was part of a practised *modus operandi*. Obviously, Jon was right about him being a bit of a wolf, but she was somehow sure he wasn't a very dangerous one.

'Please don't let me keep you from your work' Holly said, electing to stick to business. 'I just thought I'd stop by and see if I could get a tour of your laboratory some time.'

'Oh, I was just about ready to knock off, myself, and I'd be delighted to show you around. Your speciality is mycology, isn't it?'

'Yes, and I'm afraid I don't know very much about marine biology.'

'Don't apologise,' Paul said, running a hand through his hair. 'I know zilch about mycology; it's a specialist's world. Well, basically what I'm working on right now are the effects of crowding and water pollution on crabs.' He gestured to the big, neatly dissected crab that lay abdomen-up on the table. 'You know, they usually don't bother each other, but they fight like mad when they're raised in crowded pens.' He led her to three massive, blue concrete tanks filled with seawater. 'In fact, if it's during the moulting season, when their shells don't protect them, they even turn cannibalistic.'

Holly saw that one of the tanks was alive with an assortment of sea life: sluggish sea cucumbers, wavy-armed starfish, clams, mussels, skittering shrimps as transparent as glass, and a hundred other animals, half of them new to her although she'd lived on these shores all her life. The other two were filled with spider and Dungeness crabs, none of which, fortunately, were in the process of eating each other. While she marvelled at the teeming sea creatures, Paul described some of the things that made a marine biology lab unique.

'As much as possible, the environment of Sequim Bay is duplicated in these tubs. For example, the overhead lights never come on or go off suddenly. They're set by timer to reproduce the rising and setting of the sun every day—and the moon, too. And the lab is called a "wet" lab because those overhead pipes contain seawater straight from the bay. Some of them fill these tanks from the bottom, and others siphon water off from the top and return it to the bay. So the water's always circulating and always fresh.'

Holly was fascinated, but Paul looked at his watch.

'Look, I have to take the launch out and check some crab pots I set this morning.' He pointed to her brown paper bag. 'If you'd like to eat while taking a boat ride, come along.'

Holly wavered, but after being assured that she would be back before one o'clock, she assented happily, charmed by the way Paul had quickly changed gear, content to talk seriously when she hadn't responded to his opening gambit. Who could tell, maybe her plan did have a ghost of a chance of working. This man was pleasant and likeable. And wasn't liking someone the first step towards love? She brushed away the thought that no steps had been required for her to fall head over heels for Jon Alexander.

Within minutes they were speeding towards the far end of the narrow bay in the Institute's jaunty yellow-and-white launch. Holly revelled in the feel of the cool wind on her face, the view of the gleaming Institute receding among its trees, and the simple pleasure of being on the open water and away from the problems that dogged her on land. Half an hour later, she was a great deal less happy. A stray strand of giant kelp had got entangled in the propeller of the launch and it bucked to an abrupt stop, its motor revving futilely.

'Nothing serious,' Paul said cheerfully, leaning over to switch off the engine. 'I'll have us going again in a jiffy.'

Holly's heart sank. If a 'jiffy' took longer than five minutes there wouldn't be enough time left to hike up the sward and get back to the botany lab before one o'clock.

'There,' Paul said, cutting the last bit of the kelp free an agonising ten minutes later. She was going to be late on her very first day.

'What happens to people who don't get back on time from their first lunch break?' Holly asked, attempting a lightness she was far from feeling, while Paul guided the boat to a halt alongside the pier. 'Does Jon boil them in oil?'

'Let me see . . .' The marine biologist stroked his beard thoughtfully, then drawled, 'No, the last time it happened to someone, I think he just fed her to the clams.'

'Thanks for the reassurance!'

'Actually, don't worry your beautiful little head about it. Jon Alexander only drives himself endlessly, not his staff.' Paul slowly shook his head. 'He's accomplished so much you'd think he'd already proved whatever he's trying to prove. But at any rate, he's a sensitive guy and a first-rate boss; he'll understand.' Paul grinned. 'Especially when I zip up with you to do the explaining.'

'Oh, no!' Holly practically yelped. There was a definite limit to the amount she dared provoke Jon, and she'd already reached it. Colouring faintly under Paul's quizzical eye, she swiftly added, 'That really won't be necessary. He'll probably be so deep in his work he'll never even notice me.'

'You're probably right,' Paul said optimistically. 'I'd say there's a good chance of that.'

About one chance in a billion, she thought grimly, dashing up the steep stairs after hurriedly agreeing to join Paul for a drink one night after work.

Jon, his close-shaven jaw assertive, his mouth straight and hard, looked meaningfully at his watch as Holly entered the lab. Her heart sank.

'Enjoy your lunch?' he asked, steely sarcasm in his voice. 'You and Dr Keller?'

Despite Paul's assertion to the contrary, Jon Alexander looked fully capable of boiling her in oil. And as for any display of sensitivity—Holly had been given a 'Pet Rock' when the novelty gift was all the rage, and that had looked twice as sympathetic as Jon did.

Colour ran up her throat and into her cheeks,

and Holly lowered her eyes. 'I'm sorry I'm late, but——'

'Lillian's in the chemistry lab,' he interrupted. Clearly he wanted to hear no excuses. 'She left materials out for you, so you can start practising.' He turned abruptly back to his own work.

'Look, Jon, really, I couldn't help——'

'Forget it,' he shot back sarcastically. 'It's your first day in your first real job. No reason to expect you to take a professional attitude.'

Part of her was seething. Who gave him the right to nursemaid her, as he called it? What business was it of his whom she had lunch with? But another part of her—a big part—was feeling wretched. Sarcastic or not, he was right. She'd been late on her very first day, and whatever the excuse, it wasn't professional behaviour. She drove herself unmercifully all afternoon to make up for the lapse. Concentrating as fully as she could on the tasks at hand, she at least managed to win praise from Lillian.

'Nice work,' the technician said, examining Holly's slides at the end of the day. 'I think you'll be on your own by tomorrow afternoon. It's a good thing, too. Sue, the technician in the chemistry lab, is going on her maternity leave as soon as I can start filling in for her.'

Lillian's words salved Holly's conscience and helped her take Jon's brief good night with equilibrium. Then a variety of errands and chores helped take her mind off her increasingly complicated life: a run to the grocery store for groceries, exercising the dogs, and finally, wearily watering the garden. Only when she collapsed into a comfortable chair to put her feet up for a few minutes before making dinner, did things come flooding back, so that when the phone rang a few minutes later she heartily welcomed the diversion.

'Where have you been?' Anne's excited voice filled her ear. 'I've been calling every half-hour!'

'Doing errands,' Holly answered, mystified, dropping into a nearby overstuffed chair and sinking comfortably into the plump cushions. 'What's happening ... I mean, why are you so excited?'

'Excited? I'm ecstatic! And you don't have to pretend you don't know. It must have been you who told Jon Alexander I was at a loose end until my forest ranger job comes through,' Anne sighed, 'if it comes through.'

'Stop worrying. You did so well on the civil service exam they're bound to hire you. Anyway, I think I did mention it last night when he was over for dinner. He remembered you and he asked if you'd graduated too, so I——'

'*Dinner*? At *your* place? Your very first night there?' Anne was practically squeaking. 'Really? You know, I always thought——'

'Anne, let's not change the subject,' Holly interjected with mild exasperation. 'Especially not to that topic. So what happened? Did he line up a job somewhere for you?' If so, Holly thought with pleasure, it was awfully nice of him.

'Better than that. He actually *called* me and offered me a temporary job in his marine biology lab.'

'In the marine biology lab,' Holly repeated blankly, and then abruptly straightened in her chair as the light began to dawn. 'But you don't know anything about marine biology—I mean, beyond what we got in that general science class.'

'I know, but he said it didn't matter, his marine biologist could train me for what I needed to do. By the way, have you met this Paul Keller? Is he nice?' Her voice took on a faintly predatory quality. 'Is he attractive?'

'Yes to both, and he's also single, just in case you want to know, but he's supposed to be a bit of a wolf.' Holly hid a mounting anger from her friend. After all it wasn't Anne's fault that she— not to mention Holly—was being manipulated by a twentieth-century Machiavelli.

'Well, here's hoping you have your hands full with Jon Alexander, so you can leave Paul Keller for me. He sounds great.'

'I imagine that Jon has something similar in mind,' Holly said drily, 'except that what my hands will be full of is work.'

There was a confused pause on the line. 'Huh?'

'It's a long story. I'll fill you in later. When do you start work?'

'As soon as possible, he said. Tomorrow, even, but I told him I'd need a day or so to find a place to stay.'

'Don't be silly, Anne, you know I'll make room for you here.'

And so does Jon know, Holly thought, when she hung up a few minutes later. She paced furiously up and down the room. If she weren't so livid with rage, she'd have had time to admire Jon's ingenuity. In one masterful stroke, and with a single phone call, he had set in motion a chain of events that would result, on the one hand, in Holly having a roommate—in effect a chaperone—and, on the other, some very stiff competition for Paul's attention. She put out of her mind the fact that she'd already found out the marine biologist didn't attract her, not in that way, at least. But that wasn't the point. The point was that Jon Alexander, with lofty disregard for her own wishes, thought that he could interfere in her personal life whenever he felt like it. The man was just impossible! Did he think she was a puppet, and all he had to do was jerk the strings to make her dance? Well, this puppet wasn't dancing, not to *his* tune, and she was going to tell him so the minute he stuck his head out of that lab of his. And that wasn't all she was going to tell him!

It was after nine before she heard his car pull up into his driveway, but two hours had done nothing to dampen her temper.

'How dare you!' she snapped, tackling him the moment he responded to her furious thwack of the lion-headed door knocker.

Looking his calm, assured self, he smiled lazily at her. 'I rather thought you might pay me a visit tonight,' he drawled, his green eyes glinting with amusement as he ushered her into the living-room, 'but I wasn't expecting you for another ten minutes. The wine's open, but I'm afraid it hasn't had time to breathe.'

'I didn't come to make a social call, Dr Alexander,' Holly blazed. 'And it's not funny!'

He chuckled. 'Did anyone ever tell you,' he said tranquilly, 'that when you're angry your eyes scintillate like blue flames from an acetylene torch?'

'No,' she retorted, 'but then I've never been exposed very much to flights of poetic fancy.'

'Ouch.' Jon winced, still smiling, and moved to a teak bar in a corner of the living-room, on which were an opened bottle of red wine, its cork lying beside it, and two incredibly long-stemmed tulip glasses. He really *had* opened a fresh bottle of wine, damn him! He'd really, truly, been expecting her! Talk about puppets on strings!

'You don't have to pour any wine on my account,' she said in words chiselled in ice. 'All I've come for is to tell you I won't have you interfering in my private life ... I *won't*!' She'd been rehearsing just how she was going to tell him off since seven o'clock, but now her brilliant, irrefutable speech seemed to have fled from her mind.

Jon had the most aggravating way of ignoring what she said and continuing his own train of thought, and he did it now. 'Sure you won't have some?' he asked, as placid as ever. 'It's a first-rate burgundy: Château Villon.' He poured himself a glass of ruby-coloured wine. 'Mind if I sit down? I've had a hell of a day.'

Actually, there were lines of tiredness in his face, but Holly put up a quick mental barrier against the sympathy that rose so readily. He settled himself, glass in hand, in a sleek, modern chrome-and-black-leather easy chair before a wall of glass that exposed a broad, breathtaking view of twilight-lit Sequim Bay. In other circumstances, Holly could have sat silently before it for hours.

Jon put his feet up on a black-leather pouffe that matched the chair, and gracefully crossed one long leg over the other. 'Now,' he asked, in a maddeningly innocent voice, 'just how have I been interfering in your private life?'

Holly's anger soared to its summit, mainly because she felt so thoroughly silly standing in the middle of the room seething, with her fists clenched, while the object—the very deserving object—of her fury lounged in a chair, unrepentant, calmly sipping his wine and watching her in open amusement. She contemplated throwing something at him, but she knew he'd simply break into that superior laughter of his. And then she didn't know what she'd do. Try to throttle him?

'Don't play the innocent with me,' she snapped, 'and don't think I'm not able to see just how manipulative you've been, offering Anne a job.'

'Manipulative? Me?' He raised a mocking eyebrow. 'I would have thought you'd be delighted by your friend's good fortune.'

That did it. She fired a sofa pillow at him. Its trajectory was off, but still he barely rescued his wineglass before the pillow bounced off the end table.

'Hey, you need throwing lessons,' he said, laughing. 'And be careful. This is thirty-year-old burgundy you almost spilled.' He settled comfortably back in his chair. 'Tell me, Miss Fraser,' he said, suddenly professorial, 'how long have you had this strange and irresistible urge to knock over wineglasses?'

'Oh, you ... you're ... *insufferable!*' Holly sputtered, spinning on her heel.

He caught her before she could reach the door, and grasping her arms he turned her towards him. Struggling angrily, and trying hard to keep the tears at bay, Holly fought to free herself, but his powerful arms pulled her easily to his chest and pinned her helplessly there.

'Now calm down and just listen a minute,' he ordered. 'Then I'll let you go.'

She continued to struggle but the fight had gone out of her. The irresistible but strangely gentle strength of his arms, the warmth of the firm, broad chest pressed so firmly against her breasts, the compelling power of the man—all cast a spell over her that robbed her of her anger and her willpower. A few seconds ago she'd been furious, but now an almost uncontrollable hunger for him heated the deepest part of her, and she wanted nothing else but to stay in his arms for ever. God help her, why did she have to have such an unlikely love? The tears came, and Holly ducked her face and buried it against his chest so he couldn't see them sliding down her cheeks.

He said nothing for a moment, only held her, and she knew he was diplomatically ignoring her momentary weakness.

'Are you listening?' he asked finally, his voice faintly husky. The gentle stroking of her hair was closer to torture than pleasure.

'Yes,' she whispered chokingly.

'Look, I apologise. It's true; I had no right to interfere in your life. But sorry, honey, I'm afraid you're blessed—make that cursed, if you like—with being the sort of woman who brings out the protective instincts in a man. In me, anyway.'

'That's silly,' she muttered into his shirt, acutely conscious of the same clean, sandalwood scent that she remembered from his sleeping bag. 'I'm not one of those fragile little females.'

'Size has nothing to do with it.' She felt him shrug. 'Call it an air of femininity, innocence ... vulnerability. Whatever it is, I expect that even when you're sixty you'll have some man panting to take care of you.'

On principle, Holly refused to allow herself to be placated. Secretly, though, she was enchanted. He wanted to protect her ... he *cared* about her! And wasn't caring an important component of loving? Wasn't that where it sometimes started?

Unwilling to succumb to what she knew was hopeless fantasy, she spoke tartly. 'I don't need any more male protection, thank you. My brother's instincts are already as much as I can handle.' She knew her argument was rather weakened by her continuing to rest her head on Jon's chest, but she couldn't make herself move out of his embrace. However, to drive home her point more strongly, she candidly added, 'Clint didn't want me to accept the internship. He doesn't like you and he doesn't trust you.'

'I don't blame him. I'd feel exactly the same way, if I were your brother.'

Taken aback, Holly did draw her head away, and her eyes flew up to Jon's. He grinned ruefully.

'There's such a thing as masculine intuition, too, you know. We men just don't talk about it.' He forestalled the question on the tip of her tongue. 'More to the point, my protective instincts are interfering with my work. In fact, my concentration during your lunch hour was zero. So I thought of your friend. Believe me, I had no intention of just tossing Anne to the wolves ... wolf, that is. I just figured that I'd be easier in mind if there were two of you keeping tabs on each other.'

His words neatly disposed of whatever flimsy vestiges of fantasy remained. It wasn't her he really cared about at all, but only his work. How could she have been juvenile to think otherwise, even for a moment? Angrily, she pulled sharply back, her hands against his chest, and her irritation was illogically increased by the willingness with which he let go of her.

'Paul Keller isn't a wolf just because he likes women in his life,' Holly said heatedly. 'Undoubtedly, *you* see females as unfortunate biological necessities to be relegated to vacation time so they don't interfere with "important" things!' His faint flush told her she wasn't far off the mark. 'Besides, when it comes to protective instincts, if you ask me the male animal needs a lot more looking after than the female.'

Jon smiled. 'Oh?'

'Absolutely. Just because you might be able to out-box us, or you can hit a stupid ball further with a bat, doesn't mean you have enough sense to take care of yourselves. And you're a case in point: eighty-hour working weeks, sandwiches for dinner, probably no time at all available for breakfast——'

His brow wrinkled into a scowl. 'Now don't go all maternal on me,' he warned.

'How like a man!' Holly's temper was simmering again. 'The old double standard. You can mess around in my life to your heart's content, but if I seriously tried to get you to do something sensible, like eating decent meals, you'd send me packing.'

'Ordinarily, I guess I would,' Jon conceded, devilry in his eyes. 'Not tonight, though, because I sure could do with a good, home-cooked meal.' He smiled appealingly. 'I don't suppose . . .'

Holly placed one hand firmly on each hip. 'Not on your life, Jon Alexander!'

CHAPTER SEVEN

PETULANTLY, Holly yanked open the refrigerator door after Jon had taken himself off, whistling cheerily, to shower and change out of his working clothes. Did that impossible man ever fail to get his own way? When she saw what was in the refrigerator her mouth dropped open, and she stood there, astounded and bristling, at the sight in front of her. The extent of his audacity was incredible, it absolutely defied belief! He'd obviously meant to manoeuvre her into cooking dinner all along. And no wonder he'd opened up a bottle of thirty-year-old French wine. Perched on a shelf in an otherwise empty interior were two thick *filet mignons*, two lobster-tails, fresh butter, mushrooms, a solitary lemon, fresh asparagus, and a small jar of Hollandaise sauce. When she looked into the small white bakery bag she found crusty dinner rolls and two gorgeous strawberry tarts.

It would serve him right if she burnt everything to a crisp. But how could anyone deliberately ruin such food? Slamming the refrigerator door shut with a bang she hoped he could hear, she leaned back against it, shaking her head slowly back and forth, and burst out laughing. What else was there to do? The man was simply incorrigible; that's all there was to it. More relaxed, she took a good look around her for the first time.

Whoever had designed the house must have appreciated good food, because the kitchen was a dream, filled with wonderful equipment: huge, double conventional ovens, a microwave, a row of built-in food processors—three of them—a four-foot barbecue built into one of the wide, tiled counters. The contrast between the kitchen's potential and the use it got from Jon was lamentable.

She was basting the sizzling, fragrant lobster-tails with lemon butter as they slowly grilled alongside the steaks when he strolled back. At once she was glad that she had decided to change out of her jeans and into a pale green sundress and sandals before storming his door. Just why she'd done that Holly preferred not to examine; otherwise she would have felt distinctly awkward and out of place. Jon had dressed to fit the rich, casual elegance of his surroundings: cashmere sweater, silk, coral-coloured shirt and beige pants. He'd run a brush through his thick hair, but it had re-curled slightly from the shower, and she clenched her fingers against the very unmaternal urge to smooth the wayward locks down.

'I see you were able to find something,' he said blandly, appreciatively sniffing the luscious aromas from the grill. He was careful to keep any sign of gloating out of his voice, but as he looked at her busily working, with a kitchen towel tied round her waist, his mouth curved in wicked amusement. 'Anything I can do to help?'

'You can set the table,' Holly said, biting back a retort. She could see the shower had relaxed him, and it pleased her to see him looking less tired. 'And not with paper plates,' she remonstrated as she saw him pull a plastic-wrapped package out of a cupboard. 'You do have a dishwasher, you know.'

'A dishwasher with a complicated instruction manual ten pages long,' he complained. 'How am I supposed to figure out how the damned thing works?' Nevertheless, grumbling, he opened another cupboard and pulled out some formal china.

With difficulty, Holly kept herself from laughing out loud. One of the world's best scientific minds flummoxed by a dishwasher. 'Surely, one of your women friends must have offered to show you how it works?'

She was fishing and he knew it. 'My women friends all live back east. I reserve them,' he drawled, 'only for vacations.'

So she was right. He was joking—sort of—but he really did relegate women to the back shelves of his life. Like dolls to play with when he felt like taking the time. Anyway, she bet that the majority of them had no more idea than he did of how to use a dishwasher.

'I suppose you won't settle for plastic knives and forks?' His aggrieved voice cut into her thoughts.

'That's right,' she said firmly, 'and no stainless steel either. This meal deserves silver.' She had no doubt he had it, and she was right, although it took him a few moments of burrowing through cabinet drawers to discover where it was.

'How long have you been living like this?' Holly couldn't resist asking.

'Like what?' he said truculently, but he wasn't really angry. When she didn't respond he shrugged. 'Only since coming west. Back east, I usually lived in one of the family homes: Hyannisport, Sag Harbor, Georgetown . . . They're all staffed with loyal old retainers that have been there since before I was born, so I never had to worry about logistics.'

'How lovely,' she murmured, half-incredulous. 'I can't imagine what it must be like to live like that.'

Jon's visage darkened slightly. 'If, by "living like that", you mean coming from a wealthy family, it has disadvantages as well as advantages.'

'I'm sure it does,' she said, drizzling a little more butter over the lobster-tails. 'Which of the disadvantages do you find the worst?'

'The worst?' he surveyed her face, his green eyes thoughtful. 'Are you serious? Most people who aren't rich seem to think that people with money couldn't possibly have any problems at all.'

'I may not be as worldly as you are,' Holly rejoined, turning the steaks over, 'but I've experienced enough to know that everyone has problems. Logic would suggest that the rich aren't exceptions.'

'*Touché,*' he drawled, a smile playing at the corner of his mouth. Her response had pleased him . . . and his answering smile pleased her. Leaning against the tiled counter and folding his arms, he said, 'I'll tell you what the worst one is for me. No matter how stupid or lazy you are, or how intelligent and industrious, your accomplishments—or lack of them—are directly attributed to your family's money; my grandfather's in my case.' Musing, he continued, 'And the second worst is the basic assumption that if you're rich you're only playing at serious work and have no staying power.' He gave a short, hard laugh. 'Unless, of course, you're engaged in making even more money, the way my father is. Somehow, that's the only unfailingly respectable activity permitted the wealthy.'

Holly had never thought about it that way before, but it certainly made sense. She'd been guilty of a few such prejudices herself. 'I think you're right,' she said. 'People do make those assumptions.' She paused, fork in hand, and smiled. She understood a little better now why Jon had so hot-headedly left his university position without waiting for the investigation. Experience had already shown him that there would be a natural prejudice against him. 'It would be hard not to get credit when credit's due, or to always have your seriousness questioned.'

'But don't get me wrong,' Jon replied, 'there are a few little advantages to having money. I can still remember the day when my mother discovered me peering through an old, cracked magnifying glass I'd found, at some weeds I'd picked in a field near the house. I was only seven at the time, but she took me down to town that afternoon and bought me a microscope . . . not a toy either, but the best they had.' Jon grinned ruefully. 'My mother never does anything by halves. I was an only child and she spent a lot of time and attention on me. Then when my parents realised my interest in science wasn't a passing phase they picked out a prep school that had the best science programme in the US.'

'That would have given you a head start all right.'

'That wasn't all. You know those two- or three-week educational tours some of the major universities offer in the summer?'

Holly nodded. 'The kind where a professor goes along and gives lectures that a person can attend just for the fun of learning?'

'Exactly. Well, we'd go on a different one every year—a trip to the Galapagos Islands to study their flora and fauna, one to the Amazon River basin, the Swiss Alps, even one to Antarctica.'

'How fabulous,' Holly sighed. 'And I can see you now, following around whoever was in charge—the botanist, the ornithologist, the bio-logist—and picking their brains.'

Jon laughed. 'I was a bit of a pest. And of course the biggest advantage of all was that I didn't have to work my way through college the way you did.' His voice softened. 'I admire your perseverance and discipline quite a lot, you know.'

Holly blushed with pleasure, and turned from him to test an asparagus stalk with the fork. 'Even without your family's money, though, you wouldn't have had to work your way through.'

He regarded her quizzically.

'With your intellect, universities would have been fighting over you; you'd have been able to pick and choose among scholarships. And the way you took advantage of what your parents could provide counts for something too. If you'd been the kind of kid who was only interested in fooling around, or fast cars . . . why, what good would all that money have done you?'

Holly's heart flip-flopped as he walked over to her and dropped a kiss lightly on her forehead. 'Thanks for the vote of confidence.' As if he were afraid of saying more, he turned abruptly and picked up the china. 'I guess I'd better get that table set.'

By the time Jon had poured out the last drop of full-bodied wine and Holly had eaten all she could of the steak and lobster, a pleasant camaraderie had developed. Both of them were pleasantly surprised by the number of their mutual likes and dislikes: they both loved the fog and hated the summer heat; preferred their potatoes boiled rather than baked; liked old movies better than new ones; loved Chopin, hated Bartok. Holly was a little uncertain about Bartok—especially since she wasn't quite sure who he was—but if Jon didn't like him she was sure she wouldn't either. The more they talked, the more alike they found they were.

Later, when she began to clear the table, Jon went to the complicated stereo system against the stone wall at the far end of the big living-room. He inserted a tape and expertly flicked at least half a dozen switches and levers. For a man who confessed himself baffled by the complexities of an electric dishwasher, Holly reflected, smiling, he was coping pretty well.

'Chopin, of course,' he called from the living-room. '*Fantasie Impromptu.*'

He returned to the kitchen and removed a plate from her hand she was about to load into the dishwasher. Then, still holding her hand, he led her firmly into the living-room.

'We'll worry about the dishes later, after coffee and brandy. You can teach me how to use the dishwasher. Now sit down, relax, and listen to the music while I make the coffee.'

She hesitated, checked by a small warning voice inside her, but it was no match for the heady combination of delicious food, fine wine, and the glow of getting to know Jon Alexander and having him get to know her. She made for the leather chair he had sprawled in earlier.

'Not that one,' he said. 'The speaker system's focused on the centre of the room.' He pointed to the three small white sofas arranged conversationally around a free-form, glass-and-chrome coffee table. 'Try one of those.'

Obediently she went to the centre one and sank blissfully back against the soft cushions that seemed to envelop her like a warm embrace. While he busied himself in the kitchen she kicked off her sandals, put her feet up on the glass table-top— what the heck, he'd told her to relax—and lay back, letting the lovely music wash over her. Jon was certainly right about the sound. It was as if a great grand piano stood just behind her head, with Chopin himself, pale and doomed, swaying over the keyboard and sending forth that sad, beautiful, inexpressibly sweet melody. If only this could go on for ever . . .

When Jon returned with a loaded tray, he saw that she had drifted off to sleep, her hair fanned softly out around her—black as a panther's velvety fur against the textured white sofa. Her eyelids were trembling slightly, so that her thick long lashes quivered almost imperceptibly against the satiny field of her cheek, as if disturbed by some gentle breeze. Instinctively, he held his breath. For once, he felt free to take his fill of drinking in the sight of her. Panther, indeed. If he weren't careful she would creep even more deeply into his soul with all the innocent, silent stealth of a panther. And if that happened, he wasn't sure if he'd ever be able to get her out.

For a brief moment he regretted that he wasn't the marrying kind, because if he were no woman could be more perfect for him. They were, after all, both basically serious, highly motivated people who shared a common interest. And although she might be a bit overwhelmed by his lifestyle the few weeks a year he lived back east, her natural intelligence and grace would carry her through any social situation she found herself in. Combine all that with the fact that he feared he might actually be falling in love with her, and it spelled trouble with a capital T for a confirmed bachelor. What insanity possessed him to manoeuvre her into having dinner with him two nights in a row?

Irked at himself he set the tray on the coffee table with more of a clatter than was absolutely necessary, and watched her eyes flutter open at the sound. She straightened, pulling her feet off the table like a guilty child, and the spontaneous, shy

smile that illuminated her face at the sight of him
instantly wiped out his none-too-strong resolve to
take a distant chair.

'Don't get too comfortable,' he teased, lowering
himself down beside her. 'Remember, I'm depending on you to show me how that dishwasher
works.'

'I won't forget.'

With uncertainty, she eyed the brandy he
handed her. No more than a few tablespoons of
shimmering amber liquid in the bottom of a
balloon-shaped glass that must have been almost
as big as a basketball, it looked delicious, but she'd
heard it was an acquired taste and a powerful
drink. She wondered briefly if she should confess
her inexperience, but decided instead to watch how
Jon drank it, and to carefully follow suit.

Like him, she held the belly of the glass in her
hand and swirled the brandy in a slow circle, held
it up to the light and examined it (for what?),
swirled it once more, raised it, held it to her nose,
and took a deep, strong sniff——

And gasped, shuddered, choked and coughed all
at once.

'Good heavens!' she cried, when she could talk
again. 'That stuff's *lethal*! And all I did was *smell*
it!'

Laughing, and taking a sip from his own glass—
incredibly, without even making a face—he said, 'I
guess I keep forgetting what an inexperienced kid
you are in some ways.'

Those were fighting words, but Holly was too
busy wiping away the tears and catching her

breath to respond. He took her glass and, with his, set it on the table. Then he turned back to her and looked at her seriously, his eyes grave. 'Perhaps it's because you're so . . .'

She had thought nothing he could do would surprise her any more, but she was too astonished to react when he let his voice trail away, looked at her for a long moment, almost despairingly, she thought, with those deep, clear eyes, and then reached forward with both hands to pull her face to his.

It was as different from his kiss of last night as it could possibly be—not fierce and thrusting, but slow, profound, filled with gentle, insistent power that couldn't be denied. If that warning voice was still whispering, she never heard it; she wouldn't have heard it if it were bellowing. Unresisting, floating, almost unthinking, she let him pull her closer to him. Daringly, with his lips on hers, she opened her mouth; she needed desperately to be closer to him, to feel him, to taste him . . .'

He responded instantly to her invitation—she knew it was an invitation and yet she couldn't stop herself, not possibly. She felt his heartbeat accelerate, heard him catch his breath, felt it hot on her face, and she shuddered with pleasure as his tongue delved between her lips with growing passion.

Somehow, suddenly, she was lying full length on the sofa with him beside her. And when his mouth finally drew away, it was as if a deep, cold void had opened within her. But it was only to bury his face in her hair, breathing in the fragrance, pressing her head to his cheek. She shivered again, every inch of her skin tingling, as his mouth moved to her earlobes—good heavens, who could have thought earlobes could feel like that!—her cheeks, her mouth again, her throat. Excited beyond anything she thought possible by his lips, by the soft, warm puffs of his breath, by his tongue, by the long, lean length of him pressed against her, she found her hands moving urgently along his back, pressing the powerful, graceful contours of neck and shoulder muscles, and settling in the thick, short locks of hair curling at the nape of his neck, which drew her fingers like magnets.

A chill of fear broke through everything else when he slid the thin straps of her dress from her shoulders. Frightened, she brought her hands from his neck to push him away, but his lips were already moving down, brushing lightly against her collarbone, and the strength drained from her arms. Her hands lay inert against his chest, absorbing the heavy thud of his heart under her palms. The wave of passion sweeping over her robbed her not only of her strength, but of her ability to think. Sinking, moaning softly, she moved her hands again to the back of his head, pressing it closer to her, urging it down. She was almost weeping when his mouth reached her breasts, and the electrifying caress of his tongue sent such unbearably thrilling tremors through her that she groaned his name aloud.

She was barely aware that she'd done it, and entirely unaware that the effect on him was like the first sharp tick of a hair-trigger time bomb, snapping him sharply alert to danger. It was only when he abruptly sat straight up, drew her tightly into his arms, and remained perfectly still, crushing her so she could scarcely draw a breath, that she understood something had happened. He remained motionless, breathing roughly, the hammering of his heart finally beginning to slow. Holly's tears were very close to the surface now. What must he think of her? Twice in as many days she'd collapsed like a house of cards at his first touch.

She pulled away from him, tugging up the straps of her dress. 'I'm sorry——'

'Sorry!' he muttered harshly, but then his voice softened. 'Holly, this was my fault. You don't have anything to be sorry for. But you've got to learn you can't lead a man on like that.'

'But I didn't mean to *do* anything.' She was searching blindly for her shoes, the tears running down her cheeks. 'Jon, I *am* inexperienced. I've never——'

'I know that,' he said quickly. 'I guess what I mean to say is that I don't have any room in my life for a woman.' He stopped, watching her get to her feet, a fleeting smile at his lips. 'An affair's one thing; that I can handle, believe me. But you're the sort of woman a man falls in love with.'

Had she heard him right? Had he said he could fall in love with her? Was he implying that he *was* falling in love with her? Eyes shining, she opened her mouth to speak.

Jon cut her off. 'Love seems to have a way of

turning into marriage, and that's a complication that would get in the way of my work,' he said sharply, once more seeming to read her thoughts. 'And I think you know by now it's my work that's important to me, not my personal life.'

Why *isn't* your personal life important? Holly asked silently. Why shouldn't you have as much right to one as anybody else? And don't you realise your work's important to me too, and that I could help you with it, she wanted to scream at him. Then you could have me *and* your work. But he'd worked so long in his cocoon that either he wouldn't understand it or he wouldn't believe it, even if she said it out loud. It was true, she knew it, but it had to be demonstrated by action; words wouldn't do it. Her heart plummeted. How could she possibly prove it to him? She had only a single summer, a handful of weeks. But there had to be a way.

In a silence that was deafening, he walked her home along the dark path. Once she'd opened her door she stood there uncertainly, her head averted, wanting to tell him she understood him far better than he realised. But the right words wouldn't come.

He took the initiative away from her. Tilting her chin up, he forced her to look at him. To her surprise, he was smiling ruefully, his eyes gentle.

'The chemistry between us is a bit more than I can deal with, much less you. I think maybe we'd better forgo private dinner parties in the future.' He dropped a feather-light kiss on her lips and was gone.

Once inside, Holly leaned against the door, her fingers thoughtfully against lips still tingling and burning from his kisses. Could she possibly succeed—despite the lack of time, despite his determination not to get involved with her? Maybe, just maybe, she could. With all his brilliance, power, and wealth, things didn't always go Jon's way.

After all, he'd ended up getting stuck with the dishes.

As it turned out, Anne's advent on the scene turned out to Holly's advantage. Although her friend's gamine good looks and high spirits did end up captivating Paul Keller, so that by the end of the first week they were as thick as thieves, Holly didn't mind in the least. More important, Anne had willingly absorbed a great deal of the responsibility for the house and the dogs, leaving Holly free to throw herself into her work. And throw herself into it she did. It wasn't long, however, before it became dismayingly clear to her that she'd underestimated the difficulties involved in proving herself a valuable helpmate to Jon.

To begin with, she'd counted on his needing her expertise in mycology. After all, she'd been studying it diligently, almost full time, for over three years, while for him it was practically a new field. One of the few pleasant things she remembered from that awful field trip last September was how impressed he'd been with her knowledge, and how he'd relied on her. And now, she assumed happily, with the direction his research was taking, he'd need her even more. But what she hadn't counted on was his formidable intelligence. When he returned from the field trip, he'd focused his attention on the subject and in less than nine months he passed her like a high-speed express train overtaking a horse and cart out for a Sunday afternoon drive. This first-hand experiencing of his genius would have been breathtaking, if the implications of it hadn't been so depressing.

Still, if nothing else, the summer was a marvellous opportunity to learn. It couldn't help but further her career. Jon turned out to be a surprisingly patient and skilful—if demanding—teacher. He passed on so much knowledge, in fact, that she barely had time to apply it all during her normal working days, and so began experimenting with it after hours. Soon, she too had fallen into the habit of putting in twelve-hour days, sometimes more.

One advantage of this harrowing schedule, she found somewhat ironically, was that one could get so involved in learning that there was hardly any time to think, and that suited her, because when she thought, she asked herself questions she would just as well prefer not to answer, such as: What would happen to her life when the end of summer came? What would life be worth when Jon was no longer part of it?

But as the days—and the long evenings—passed, other questions began to emerge and set her mind racing once again: If she continued to work this hard, and learn this much, why *shouldn't* he come to count on her after all? Why shouldn't he see what she might mean to him—helper, friend . . . wife, even?

At first she expected her extended days to pass unremarked, because she seriously doubted if Jon, with his remarkable powers of concentration, would notice a herd of trumpeting elephants passing through the lab, much less her silent presence in the otherwise deserted Institute. But in the second week of her internship, he looked up one night, glanced at his watch, and grumbled, 'It's after seven. What are you doing here?'

'Working, what does it look like?' she retorted lightly, brushing back a wisp of hair that had worked loose from her chignon.

He scowled at her. 'Well, if it's part of a plot to make me feel like a slave driver, or if you and Lillian have put your heads together to show me what long hours *I* do, you can forget about it. It won't work.'

Holly threw him a dark look in return. 'I don't suppose it's ever occurred to you that I might be interested enough in what I'm learning and in my own career,' she said haughtily, 'to put in a few extra hours out of sheer interest.'

There was enough conviction in her voice to convince him she meant it, but still she breathed a sigh of relief at the grunt that appeared to signify his grudging acquiescence. For the truth was that there was yet another reason for these long evening hours.

They were the only time she felt free to let her own concentration slip just a little from time to time. She'd wait until his attention was riveted on his microscope or computer terminal, and then let her eyes drift to fix on him. Those moments of gazing at him unobserved filled her with a precious, painful pleasure—the sort of thing that drew a child with a ten-cents-a-week allowance to the window of a toy store for the 'enjoyment' of looking at a hundred-dollar bicycle.

Unfortunately, never once when she'd looked up had she found him gazing with any longing at her, or gazing at all, for that matter. Men certainly seemed to be irritatingly successful at burying their feelings when it suited them. Certainly Jon Alexander was an all-time champion at it.

Mostly, though, Holly put her extra hours to good use—so much so that by the last week in July she was desperately in need of a breather. Her head was so full of new information that she was afraid that if she tried to absorb another new fact, or one more new equation, the nerves in her brain would short-circuit and fizzle out in a puff of smoke.

Happily, there was a weekend just ahead, and she intended to use it for nothing but relaxing. And, this being late on a Friday afternoon, she was going to start right now. She stood up and stretched, rubbing the back of her tired neck, then took off her white lab coat and tossed it in the laundry bin. At the door she hesitated for a moment, debating whether or not she ought to lock up the laboratory. Jon had been closeted all day with his accountant, who had arrived early that morning from Seattle. Might as well, she decided, they must still be hard at it. She was just pulling the door closed behind her when she saw Jon striding down the hall in her direction.

Halting, the door ajar, she said, 'I'm off ... Shall I leave it open for you?'

'Yes ... No.' He ran a distracted hand through his hair—obviously not for the first time that day, since it was a good deal more dishevelled than usual. 'It's been a hell of a day, and I doubt if I'd get anything productive done tonight anyway.' He jammed his hands in his pockets as they walked together down the corridor. 'I guess I'll use the time to put in a few hours on the article I'm writing. What about you? Going home at a normal hour for a change?'

'Well, not home. Anne and Paul have talked me into a beach dinner picnic.' She glanced at her watch. 'They should be out on his boat right now, hauling in the crab pot.'

'Fresh cracked crab on the beach,' he said wistfully. 'That sounds good.'

'You could always put off your writing and join us,' Holly said, with no real hope for an affirmative answer. During the last two months she'd learned that he hadn't exaggerated in the slightest about not having time for much of a social life.

'I guess I could, couldn't I?' he said to her surprise. 'What shall I bring?'

A glint of humour leaping into his eyes told her that her astonishment and delight must have shown in her face, although she'd thought she'd managed to keep her expression steady.

'Just bring yourself—about seven. There'll be plenty to eat even if the crabs aren't biting. Anne and I bought some chicken to barbecue as a back-up.'

Holly drove home on a cloud, freshly determined to enjoy the evening before her. She would bask in the unaccustomed pleasure of Jon's company outside the lab, but she wasn't going to give way to doubts and fears for the future. And no thoughts about career or work either—nothing but a long, midsummer twilight in which to savour food, friends, and utter relaxation. Tonight, for once, she was going to live in the present.

When she got to the house she stepped out on to the wooden veranda and looked down the forest-rimmed length of Sequim Bay, a long finger of aquamarine, alive with glittering, dancing reflections of the evening sun. She could just make out Paul's boat, the *Wandering Tattler*, bobbing gently offshore. Until he and Anne returned with their catch, if any, she wouldn't know whether to make coleslaw—the perfect accompaniment for a cracked crab dinner—or a mixed green salad that would go better with barbecued chicken. That meant she had time to take a long, cool bath and wash her hair, which would be a lovely way to start the weekend. She waltzed half-way to the bathroom, then stopped and dashed to the telephone. She'd almost forgotten to phone Clint.

'How's Mary?' she asked anxiously, as soon as her brother answered. The final prenatal check-up had been scheduled for that morning.

'A lot more relaxed than I am, fortunately,'

Clint joked. 'Dr Morehead says she's doing fine, and that it'll be only a week or so now before the baby comes.'

'Fine,' Holly said, relieved. 'Now, remember, you promised to call me, day or night, as soon as she goes into labour.'

'Okay, but I hope it's not two o'clock in the morning,' he grumbled. 'I don't like the idea of you driving that old banger of yours to the hospital in the middle of the night.'

Holly smiled. Even in the midst of being the anxious husband, he couldn't quite give up playing the ever-watchful big brother. 'You don't have to worry. If it's really late I'll borrow Anne's car. Her dad's rebuilt the engine, and it runs like new.'

'Okay, good,' Clint said, his voice lightening. 'Let me tell you, I'm a lot happier about your working at that place since Alexander hired Anne. You know, I may have misjudged the guy.'

Holly was pleased. She wanted Clint to like Jon. 'I think you did,' she said eagerly. 'He's a fantastic person once you get to know him more intimately.'

Clint's mumbling mutter, uninteligible as it was, told her that her choice of words had been less than fortunate, and that Clint, even if he were softening, was hardly an ardent fan of Jon Alexander's. It was a case, she thought with a mixture of amusement and exasperation, of one dyed-in-the-wool male chauvinist recognising a kindred spirit and being put off by it. Rather like the way one big, ferocious dog reacts to another— circling it warily, its fur bristling, thinking about being friends, but just as ready to go for the throat. Men!

'So,' Clint said, shifting the subject, 'how's your work going?'

Here was something they could both be enthusiastic about, and in her eagerness to fill him in on the latest details she forgot completely about the time. When she finally put down the telephone a glance towards the bay showed her that the *Wandering Tattler* was already making for shore. No time for a leisurely bath after all, and she had barely finished blow-drying her hair after a quick shower when the dogs' excited, friendly barking alerted her to the arrival of the crabbing party. Hurriedly slipping into a pair of worn jeans and lavender T-shirt (Jon certainly wouldn't be able to claim she was out to vamp him), she got downstairs just as Paul and Anne entered, carrying between them a plastic tub containing at least six huge Dungeness crabs.

'Wow!' Holly exclaimed as they set it on the draining-board next to the sink. 'You've really had some luck!'

'Luck?' Paul said, striking a humorously offended pose. 'I don't know about that. *One* of us caught our limit, but the other one—who shall remain nameless—barely managed to come up with two; one of which was a female, and the other of which was an undersized male, so we had to throw both of them back.'

Anne, her hazel eyes dancing with indignation, playfully snapped a kitchen towel at him. 'Sure, but some sportsman you are!' Tossing her brown curls, she turned to Holly, 'While I was working hard at luring them with a baited crab pot, *he* put on his scuba gear, dived in, and just picked the creatures off the bottom. Talk about an unfair advantage!'

Unabashed, Paul cheerfully set about cleaning the crabs.

'Whatever the method,' Holly said, smiling, 'I'm glad you had such a successful trip. By the way,' she added, trying to sound casual, 'I've invited Jon over and he's accepted. I hope you don't mind.'

'Jon? Of course not,' Anne answered, pleasure and surprise in her voice. Holly could see she was bursting with questions, but was holding them—at least until they were alone. 'There's more than enough.'

'True, but due only to my vastly superior skill and ingenuity,' Paul intoned sanctimoniously, his brown eyes twinkling. Then, laughing, he ducked as Anne went at him with the towel again.

Holly, watching him dodge nimbly around the kitchen counter and out of Anne's reach, laughed too, but it was marred just a little by a faint twinge of jealousy. With what ease and laughter Anne's relationship with the marine biologist was developing. Holly wouldn't be surprised if things turned serious between those two, and, as far as she could see, there weren't any self-imposed obstacles in their path. But then, she thought philosophically, as she took the cabbage from the refrigerator and starting chopping it for the coleslaw, they were different people from her and Jon, so comparisons were futile. Besides, she'd

promised herself there would be no morbid
ruminations tonight. Tonight it was 'Gather ye
rosebuds while ye may . . .'

The portable freezer box was crammed to
capacity with food by the time Jon arrived, but
somehow Anne managed to tuck in the bottle of
white wine he brought. Then he and Paul, carrying
the box between them, with a folded beach blanket
on top of it, set off on the trail down to the beach,
with Holly and Anne following, their arms loaded
with the coats that all would need when the sun set
in a couple of hours.

Jon, easily adapting himself to the others'
bantering mood, helped Paul build a fire while the
women unpacked and arranged the food. After an
obligatory conversation about how they really
should take a walk before dinner, followed by
quick rationalisations to the effect that it really
made more sense to eat first, the four of them dug
in ravenously.

An hour later they settled happily back against
some driftwood logs they'd hauled over to make
back-rests.

'What a feast,' Jon said contentedly, eyeing
the debris with satisfaction. 'A swarm of car-
penter ants couldn't have polished it off any
better.'

'I won't be able to eat again for a week,' Anne
sighed. 'I'm stuffed.' But with no apparent difficulty
she swallowed the last bite of her second chocolate
brownie.

Paul rose, then pulled a reluctant Anne to her
feet. 'All you need is a good walk.' He turned

to Jon and Holly. 'Coming? We can clean up later.'

'To be honest,' Holly admitted, 'I couldn't move right at this moment even if I wanted to, so I'll take care of the clearing-up ... in a few minutes. But you three go on.'

To her intense pleasure, Jon said, 'I'll stay and lend Holly a hand. As soon as I can move.'

'Did your accountant finish his audit?' she asked conversationally a few minutes later, as she repacked the now empty plastic containers.

'Yes, and delivered his usual lecture,' Jon replied drily. He tossed the paper plates into the fire and watched them puff into flame, his brow creased. 'A research facility is damned expensive to maintain ... something old Grayson feels obliged to point out rather vehemently every time he adds up the previous six months' outlay—as if I didn't already know.'

'And pure research doesn't pay its own way, does it?' Holly said thoughtfully. 'In money, I mean.'

Jon shrugged indifferently. 'Money's not really the problem, even if Grayson thinks it is. I'm not exactly poor, you know, and so far I've been lucky with investments; enough to carry the Institute and——' he smiled faintly, '—support myself in the style to which I'm accustomed. And I think my resources will last until we've accomplished at least some of our goals. The question is whether *I'll* last.'

He peered moodily into the snapping fire, his face lit by the orange flames. His eyes were distant, the strong lines and angles of his face tense. 'It's not the research; I can handle that. Nobody in the world could do it better.' This was stated not with arrogance, but as a simple, obvious truth. 'It's the administration that's getting to me—the details. The lousy, trivial details.'

He spoke quietly, seeming to address the fire, but with intensity and frustration so tangible that Holly felt it as her own. With startling clarity she realised that she hadn't even begun to understand what a tremendous weight of responsibility he carried. His research work was only half of it. She hadn't given a thought to the administrative aspects of running a front-rank research institute with a staff of sixty. Now that she did think about it, he spent no more than half of his time in the lab itself. There were budget meetings, planning sessions, flying trips to Chicago and Berkeley, an appearance before a United Nations' sub-committee—activities that had seemed exciting to her, but were irritating, time-destroying 'details' to him. No wonder he was sometimes in the lab at midnight, and occasionally even spent the night on the bed in his office.

She thought back to Dr Kirkland's words. '. . . he's a renegade, still doing it on his own rather than co-operating with the academic establishment.' How naïvely Holly had admired his independence. Now she realised her ex-professor was right. How much more he could accomplish if he had a major university behind him, with loads of money—the kind that only a great institution, with its grants, foundations, and networks has—

and a legion of adminstrators to take care of all the 'details'. He could devote his entire day to research, with a phalanx of the very best postgraduate students in the country to help him, and the stimulation of university colleagues as well. Why, he could have time for a regular social life—a family life, even.

But how could she possibly broach the subject to him without his finding out that Dr Kirkland had told her about his past? Holly had promised she wouldn't breathe a word. And would he listen to her anyway? Not likely.

'How about that walk now?' Jon said, cutting into her thoughts. 'Then, as pleasant as this has been, I do have to get down to that article.'

A long, relaxing weekend of mindless sleeping-in, exercising, and relaxing with an Agatha Christie novel was just what Holly had needed and by Sunday night she was cheerfully looking forward to jumping back into the fray.

The telephone at her bedside rang at a little after eleven, just as she was reaching out to switch off the reading light. She knew what it was about before she picked up the receiver.

'It looks like the little rascal decided to come a week early,' her brother said. 'As soon as Mary finishes getting ready, we're off to the hospital.'

'Everything's all right, isn't it?' Holly knew her brother too well not to note the underlying anxiety in his voice.

'Mary's doing fine,' Clint hastened to assure

her. 'She's fussing because she can't find her knitting.'

Then Holly remembered. 'Oh, no—you have to go to that three-day conference at the Grand Canyon, don't you? Starting on Tuesday!'

'Well, I'll just have to miss it, no big deal,' Clint replied matter-of-factly, but he wasn't fooling Holly. She knew that only one ranger per national park had been selected to go, and it was not only an honour to be invited, but an enormous career boost to be directly involved in some of the long-term decisions that were to be made. 'Mary's mum has a heck of a cold,' he continued, 'so she can't help with the baby, and of course I'm not going to leave Mary alone.'

'Of course you can't leave her alone,' Holly said, climbing out of bed. 'There's *me*. I'm on my way. See you at the hospital.'

'But what about your job?'

'I'll just take a week off, that's all.'

'But will your boss let you . . . I mean . . .'

'This is an emergency. Jon will just have to understand,' Holly said firmly, rather enjoying being the solid, sensible 'big' sister for once. And as far as her boss went, it was doubtful that she'd even be missed, she thought ruefully as she dialled Jon's home number.

She made a wry face into the telephone receiver when he promptly assented to her absence. At least he could have pretended he'd miss her help, if nothing else.

'I might be able to make it back by Friday,' she said hopefully. 'Monday at the latest.'

'No rush, take your time,' was the airy response. 'Oh, and congratulate the parents for me.'

Holly barely resisted the impulse to stick her tongue out at the receiver after he hung up. 'Honestly, Jon Alexander, one of these days . . .'

CHAPTER EIGHT

HOLLY had brought along some botanical text-books and journals, for her new nephew—a fascinating, round little scrap of humanity that she could have watched for ever, even when he was sleeping—kept her busy through the day. But the books were good companions for those long night hours when she needed distraction from the obsessive thoughts of Jon that had crowded back into her mind. The summer was passing quickly—most of it was gone—and here she was far from the Institute, with no way of proving to Jon how helpful she could be to him. Not that he seemed overwhelmingly aware of it even when she was there. No, she had to admit to herself that she wasn't a whit closer to her goal than she'd been two months ago.

'You mean that tome hasn't put you to sleep yet?' Mary marvelled one night when she got up for a one a.m. feed and discovered Holly still reading in an armchair in the living-room.

'Not at all,' Holly said uncurling her legs and straightening up. 'In fact, I'm so excited I couldn't possibly sleep. I've just got the germ of an idea . . . a new approach, really, to an experiment that I was running for Jon.'

The baby was unimpressed by these momentous words. With tiny fist waving, and his face turning as crimson as his few wisps of red hair, he interrupted the conversation with an ear-piercing wail that said in no uncertain terms that it was mealtime and botanical experiments could wait.

Mary and Holly looked at each other and laughed, remembering how the nurses at the hospital had claimed after a mere twenty-four hours, that Clint Junior would never need lessons in assertiveness. How right they were!

'Why don't you make us some hot chocolate while I start feeding this little fellow?' Mary said, settling with the baby into the rocking-chair. 'Then I want to hear all about it.'

An hour later, after Holly had carefully explained her idea, Mary commented thoughtfully, 'It does sound like you might have something there.' She chewed on her bottom lip and stared reflectively down at her sleeping, chubby son. 'The concept sounds so . . . uncomplicated, though. If it was that simple, wouldn't Jon have tried it a long time ago?'

'Possibly,' Holly admitted, 'but not necessarily. Novices have a way of coming up with simple, direct approaches because they don't have so many preconceived ideas. But seasoned researchers can get so caught up in complexities that the easy solutions just don't occur to them. Especially when they work in isolation, like Jon.'

'In isolation? Doesn't he have other scientists working for him?'

'Yes, a chemist and a marine biologist, plus a support staff—technicians, mostly—but no other professional botanists.'

'I hadn't realised that,' Mary replied, 'and I suppose you interns aren't there long enough to help much?'

'Right. And I think he seem the internship programme as a kind of civic duty, not as a help to him.' Holly rolled her eyes to the ceiling. 'I can just imagine how much arm-twisting they had to do to get him to sponsor it.' She didn't think she'd be violating a confidence to add, 'Jon doesn't think too much of the academic world. I guess that's why he doesn't even socialise with Dr Kirkland, just a few houses down.'

'I see,' Mary said thoughtfully. 'Since he's working without other botanists to toss around ideas with, he doesn't get the benefit of their influence, their . . .'

'Cross-fertilisation,' Holly said, laughing. 'I think that's the right word for botanists.'

Mary was serious. 'And that means you really might be on to something he never thought of. How exciting!'

Holly smiled. ' "Might" is the word, all right. My idea might also be all wet. I'll just have to wait until I get back to the lab and try it out on Jon.'

Since Clint didn't make it back home until late Friday afternoon, Holly decided she might as well spend the weekend at Lake Quinault so she could help out a little longer and also hear all about the conference, even though she was champing at the bit to return to work . . . and dying for just a sight of Jon. So, instead of returning to Sequim on Sunday evening when the traffic would be slowed by weekenders pulling trailers and boats behind them as they headed home from the peninsula for Seattle, Holly started off in the quiet hours just before dawn on Monday morning.

With only a brief stop at McDonald's in Port Angeles for a big cup of steaming black coffee and an Egg McMuffin she managed to pull into the Alexander Institute car park at only a few minutes after eight.

So glad was she to get back that she forced herself to pause for a moment before going in to remind herself gravely that it was merely a temporary job she was returning to, and just because she'd been missing him didn't mean he'd been missing her. And in a mere three weeks, in all likelihood, she would be parted from him for ever. Sobered, but only for an instant, and not by much, she ran irrepressibly on, elated at the thought of being near him again. Three weeks were three weeks and anything might have happened. He overworked, didn't he? And hadn't he told her the administrative work was getting him down? Who could tell, he might get sick, and she could nurse——

A bellow as irate as a bull's, and twice as healthy, put a prompt end to that line of thinking.

'Well, damn it . . .! Use some initiative! Call her brother's house in Quinault and find out if she's still there!'

Holly heard a book slam down on a table just as a visibly shaken Lillian shot out of the door of the lab like a doe running before a forest fire.

Practically skidding to a halt when she caught sight of Holly, the technician breathed a huge sigh of relief and hurried to her.

'Thank God you're here,' she whispered. 'He's been snarling and snapping since last Tuesday, but when you didn't come in on Friday,' she raised her eyes ceilingward 'he became absolutely *impossible*.'

'You're kidding,' Holly responded in disbelief. 'He told me to stay until today if I wanted.'

'Well, if he did, it obviously slipped his mind.' Lillian compressed her thin lips together and shook her head. 'In all my years here, I've never seen him act like this. I'd hate to be in your shoes right at this minute.'

In a state of mild shock, Holly warily entered the lab. Her spine actually tingled with a touch of panic when an angry, almost savage Jon Alexander turned on her.

'Where the hell have you been?' he yelled. 'You were supposed to be back on Friday.'

'I said I'd try to be back on Friday,' Holly corrected in a placating tone which had no effect whatever, 'but that Monday would be more like it.'

'Well, you should have tried harder.' He stood up and tossed some notes crossly on the bench. 'Just how the hell did you expect me to get any work done around here while you were gone?'

'The same way you got work done before me!' she flared, abandoning diplomacy in the wake of this maddeningly unjustified indignation. 'You told me yourself that Lillian could handle my work . . . and that it was perfectly okay for me to take my time.'

'Well, that's what I thought,' he muttered curtly in a muffled voice, which rose again as he ground out, 'but that was before I realised just how sneakily you'd wormed your way into my experiments.'

Holly stared at him incredulously. Sneakily . . .? Wormed her way . . .? She hadn't been doing anything he hadn't taught her—indeed, encouraged her—to do.

'I'm an intern, remember, not just a lab technican,' she snapped, literally seeing red at his tone and his insinuation, 'and the whole idea is for me to start learning the job responsibilities of a botanist——'

'Neither of the last two interns developed beyond technician level, so——'

'Is it *my* fault they didn't take advantage of their situation?' she interrupted haughtily. 'As for me, I was trying to get all of the practical experience I could before I start postgraduate studies.'

But of course that wasn't all she'd been trying to do. As furious as she was with him, she realised he was right. She'd practically worn herself out trying to become indispensable to him. Had she succeeded without knowing it? She suppressed a rising thrill of excitement. This was no time to let Jon in on her scheme. Besides he had no right to bark at her like this. You'd have thought she'd sabotaged him, not proved herself helpful.

At her mention of postgraduate studies, Jon's face had darkened further, but now his anger subsided to a steady simmer and his grey-green eyes sardonically took in her flushed skin, brilliant eyes, and piqued mouth.

'And I suppose,' he said, 'you can't wait to run

out on me at the end of the summer so you can go and become a star pupil at some university.'

'I can't believe how unfair you're being,' she gasped. He was not only unfair, he was utterly impossible.

With an impatient movement, Jon rammed his hands into the pockets of his lab coat, turned away from her slightly for a moment, then whirled back just as abruptly.

'Unfair?' How fair is it for you to turn my lab routine upside down, to introduce a hundred little improvements, to make me depend on you—while all the time you're planning to skip out in the autumn?'

Her eyes opened wider. In a way he had a point, except, of course, that 'skipping out' was the last thing in the world she wanted to do.

'All right, that's enough,' he said, dismissively waving his hand, as if she wanted to continue the argument. 'I've wasted too much time already this morning. Where are the mycorrhizal specimens you were working on the week before last? Nobody can figure out where the hell you put them.'

Subdued, confused, feeling slightly guilty, she hastened to show him. She'd have felt worse still if not for the odd fact that Jon hadn't telephoned her even once last week to ask where anything was, which he could easily have done. Had he deliberately let his anger and irritation grow? But why?

They both busied themselves in near silence for the rest of the day, but Holly was aware of a definite change in Jon—an absence of his usual ability to immerse himself in his work. Even more interesting, she had more than once looked up to find his eyes on her. The crackling tension in the air was so palpable, however, that she was forced to drop her own glance each time. Visual duels with those lancing green eyes were something she wasn't ready for.

When he stopped at her bench a little after five, she looked up, swallowing nervously.

'Is there something you can't find?' Faint colour mantled her cheeks as his frankly assessing eyes travelled over her face.

'Put those things away,' he ordered brusquely. 'I want to talk to you, and I don't want to do it here.'

She returned her blue specimen trays to the incubator unit, making herself take her time. She even thought about giving in to her instinctive desire to dig in her heels and refuse to budge until he converted his command into a civil request. But curiosity got the better of her.

'Where are we going?' Holly asked, as he steered her car towards the car park exit.

'My place.' His challenging look set her heart thumping. 'Any objections?'

As if it mattered, she thought, looking at the belligerently masculine line of his jaw. Taking her silence as assent he nodded curtly and continued on. Neither of them spoke during the rest of the short drive to his house.

Once inside he made for the bar to make himself a drink. 'Would you like something?' he called over his shoulder as an afterthought. 'Sherry?'

'Sherry would be fine.' She didn't want anything to drink but she was on pins and needles, and it would give her something to do with her hands.

She accepted the fluted glass and sat down in one of the leather easy chairs while he stood at the big window, sipping the Scotch he'd poured for himself, and scowling moodily at the placid waters of the bay.

Her nerves were stretched wire-tight by the tensions of the day, by the growing, sickening fear that without thinking she'd done him harm, and she was on the verge of speaking, when he turned. The anger, she saw at once, had burnt out of him.

'If I had any sense, I'd fire you,' he said, without preamble. 'I had no idea I'd got so used to your help in the lab, and to . . .' His gaze, usually so direct, dropped to his glass. She heard a soft tinkle of ice as his hand moved slightly. '. . . to . . . well, to just having you there—near me.'

She peered at him with startled eyes, trying unsuccessfully to read his expression. When he looked suddenly up to see her studying him, he set down his drink and moved swiftly across the room to her. Unbelievably, she found herself being pulled upright into his arms, her head swimming. Was the impossible really happening?

'I was pretty successful at resisting you at first,' he murmured into her hair. 'Your still being at college made it pretty easy, and I managed to push you to the back of my mind after the field trip——'

'Out of sight, out of mind . . .' she interjected dazedly.

He gave a husky laugh. 'Something like that,' he said, gently stroking the long, silken strands of her hair. 'But from the minute you walked into my office, looking so damn cool and professional . . . so achingly beautiful . . . I've just been fighting the inevitable. I thought I was strong enough to resist the feelings I had for you—after all, it would only be for a summer. But I enjoyed teaching you a lot more than I thought I would, although it wasn't until this last week that I realised how much you'd learned and how much I'd grown to depend on you . . .' He chuckled. '. . . and how I'd been digging my own trap, so to speak.'

His arms tightened around her. 'I love you, Holly,' he added, rough and tender both, 'and I want you.'

'Jon . . .' Just thinking of how close she'd come to pridefully refusing to apply for the internship made the blood freeze in her veins. She pulled her head back so she could look up at his face. Eyes glowing, barely able to speak, she had to hear it again. 'Do you really mean that? You love me?'

'God help me, I do . . . Although I don't quite know what I'm going to do with you . . .'

'I can work with you in the lab and——'

He stopped her with a short, eager kiss. 'Right now, though, you're more distraction than you're worth,' he teased. 'I suppose we could always get married . . .'

Holly threw her arms around his neck. 'Of course we could! Oh, Jon . . . When?'

'Whenever you say. Today!'

'Today?'

'All right, then,' he said laughing, 'I wouldn't want to rush you. How about tomorrow?'

'Tomorrow?' she repeated vaguely. 'But . . . it's so . . .'

She felt him stiffen. 'What's wrong, Holly?'

'Nothing's wrong. It's only that . . . nothing.'

He pulled her arms gently from his neck and held her a little away from him so he could get a clear view of her face. 'Don't tell me "nothing".' His forehead was creased, his eyes full of angry bafflement. 'I can hear something in your voice—a pulling-back.'

'Oh, no!' she cried hotly. 'You're wrong!'

But he wasn't. She had heard it too, in her own voice—not a pulling-back, exactly, but a sense of reticence, of indecision. What in heaven's name was happening? The incredible had come true. Jon Alexander had just asked her to marry him . . . and she was suddenly filled with reservations! Perplexed, befuddled, she tried to examine her own mind. Had the week away from him changed her, had those long, peaceful hours of watching Clint and Mary cooing absurdly over their baby and holding hands before the fire for whole evenings at a time somehow——

'I'm not wrong,' Jon persevered. 'What are you telling me? That you're not sure you love me?'

'Of . . . of course not,' she stammered. 'I love you with all my heart, and I always will. I just meant that . . . that . . .'

He stared steadily at her with eyes that were chillingly remote, not speaking, not even trying to help her sort out her own muddled feelings. She *did* love him with all her heart; all she wanted to do at this very minute was to wrap her arms around him again and fold his hurt, puzzled face to her breast. And yet . . .

'Jon . . . darling . . . all I mean was that I realise it'll take a little while for you to arrange things so we can have time together. I understand how all-consuming your work is right now and——'

'Right now?' he exploded. 'I'm *never* going to have any more time than I do right now!' Coldly, he dropped his hands from her arms. 'I thought you understood how important what I'm doing is.' He ran his fingers distractedly though his hair, and Holly longed to smooth it for him with her fingers. 'Hell, I thought you cared about it, too—otherwise I'd never even thought about marriage.' His eyes were still on hers, but he seemed no longer to be looking at her. 'I guess I was wrong.'

'I *do* care about your work—tremendously,' Holly insisted desperately. 'You must know that! I'd never dream of asking you to give it up——'

Her throat was clogged with emotion, so that the confused, distraught words stuck painfully in her chest. How could this be happening? Why were they arguing? How could her dream turn so suddenly into a nightmare? Struggling for coherent words she went on frantically.

'It's not the research—I *want* you to keep on with that—I want to *help* you, if you'll let me—I just thought you'd need a little time to arrange . . . to pass on some of the administrative details that take up so much of your——'

'And just how do you propose I do that?'

'Surely there are universities that would be glad to have you as——'

'Forget it.' He turned away from her, walked to the window, and stared broodingly out. 'I want nothing to do with them.'

'Jon, I realise that what happened years ago——'

He threw her a dark look over his shoulder. 'So you know about that, do you?'

'Not the details, just that there'd been a problem——'

'A problem,' he repeated, and laughed humourlessly. 'A slut who skulked into my house one night when I was working at the library, and drank half a bottle of my Scotch—to get her nerve up, I suppose. I came home to a very drunk, very amorous undergraduate.'

'What happened then?' she asked quietly, praying that if he talked about it some of the bitterness he had held inside him for so long would dissolve. And perhaps if they just kept talking they could close the frightening rift that had opened so unexpectedly between them.

'Before I had a chance to work out how to get her out of there, the dean dropped by with a question. And as soon as she saw him—or he saw her, rather—she burst very convincingly into tears, ran hysterically to him, and accused me of ... well, you can guess.' He shrugged. 'That was all. The next morning papers were being prepared for an academic senate hearing. The charges started with moral turpitude and went on from there.'

'Oh, dear ... But no one could have believed her in the end, because the hearing vindicated you.'

He frowned. 'It sounds to me as if you know quite a few of the details. I suppose Kirkland's been gossiping. That's a surprise.'

Holly shook her head vehemently. 'It wasn't like that at all. She admires you and respects you, and she thinks it's been really unfortunate for the academic world, and for you too, that——'

'Well, next time you see her,' he cut in scornfully, 'you can tell her not to worry about it on my account. I haven't lost anything worth having.'

'But you have,' Holly rejoined. 'Can't you see how much time you lose from your research by having to run your own facility instead of letting a university administer it for you? All those "details" you have to take care of? And then there's your research itself. You must know better than I how dangerous it is for you to work in isolation, without colleagues in your own field to bounce ideas off and to get ideas from. You'd find them in a university faculty. And just think of what it would mean if you could be passing your knowledge on to a dozen—two dozen—top postgraduates instead of a single intern!'

With the back of her hand she brushed at suddenly briming tears. 'And—oh, Jon—they'd be so much more helpful than I am because I can't keep up with you. I can't work and work the way you do, or live the way you live. I don't have your brilliance, your strength . . .'

She sighed, drained. The flood of words had exhausted her. If nothing else, it had helped her to understand her own jumbled feelings a little better.

But from the set of his shoulders she could see that it had had no effect on Jon. He seized obstinately on her words.

'Because I put in long hours doesn't mean I would have expected you to.'

She gave a helpless little shrug. 'And what would I do while you were working to eleven o'clock ... to midnight?' The tears began to flow again but this time they ran unchecked down her cheeks. 'Wander around this big, empty house, preparing meals I'd have to eat alone? Look at television until I was too tired to stay up and then go to bed by myself?'

'I guess this isn't getting us anywhere,' he said in a voice devoid of everything but weariness. 'Let's just forget I ever brought it up.'

On that note he turned on his heel, left the room and then walked out of his own house, slamming the front door behind him. A few moments later she heard his car start up ferociously and roar off into the night.

CHAPTER NINE

'FINISHED with the report?' Lillian asked poking her head in at the laboratory door.

Holly stopped writing, looked up, and shook her head. 'I'll need at least another half-hour.' She smiled, but it was a hollow smile that didn't show in her eyes. 'If it misses the mail pick-up, I'll drive it to the post office myself.'

After the lab technician left, Holly chewed thoughtfully on the end of her pen. Should she include something on the progress of her little experiment, even though she'd never got Jon's permission to try it?

Not that she could have if she'd wanted to. The thought set off the dull ache that had sat just behind her eyes since that horrible scene a week and a half ago. After a night of weeping and torturing herself with self-reproach (why hadn't she just married him on the spot and worked out any problems later?) Holly had shown up at the Institute the next morning to hand in her resignation and collect the personal things she kept in the lab. She had fretted over just how she could avoid seeing him, and what she would say if that were impossible, but she needn't have worried. Jon had left even earlier for parts unknown.

Lillian had clucked her disapproval, 'Usually, when he goes on a trip he at least gives me a few days' warning and a return date. What could have made him leave so suddenly?' As she took in Holly's shaken demeanour and the obvious signs of a sleepless night, her eyes softened knowingly. 'I suppose some research emergency took him away. There are a lot of those.'

'I suppose so,' Holly echoed faintly, appreciating Lillian's tact. 'Did he ... did he leave any messages for me?'

'Just for you to carry on as well as you could.'

'Me?' Holly gasped. 'Carry on? Why I couldn't ...' How unfair of him to ask her! To force on her the torture of touching his things, working on alone in the lab when every single thing she did would remind her of him—while he just took off and ran away from it all.

Lillian frowned worriedly. 'But there isn't anyone else right now who could possibly take over. Sue can't return yet, so I'm still needed in the chemistry lab. And besides, I don't know anything about those tests you've been running on the mycorrhizoids.'

Holly's lips tightened. She was trapped. Jon had been wrong about one thing at least. She did care fervently about what his work meant to the world. And she cared about her own efforts on behalf of it. There were several tests that had to be charted twice daily and maintained almost continuously or the experiments in progress would have to be abandoned and started again. Months of Jon's work might go down the drain if she walked out. Not that it wouldn't serve him right, but ...

'You're right, of course, Lillian,' Holly said,

suppressing her anger and frustration. 'Did he leave any special instructions?'

'Only that he'd appreciate progress reports on all experiments every week or so. We're to send them to his family's home at Sag Harbor, and they'll forward them on to him—wherever he'll be.'

That had been ten days ago, and the first of her reports was overdue. Yes, she decided suddenly, she would include an account of her private experiment. Why not? She was proud of it. The idea that had come to her out of the blue while staying with Mary and the baby had been a godsend. Only by working until she was about to drop had she been able to get through the days—if not the nights—reasonably tranquilly. And if her idea was silly, let him go ahead and laugh. What did she care?

Not allowing herself to answer that one, she returned to her report, cogently describing what she'd been doing, and then enumerating the data so far—data which looked quite promising, to her at any rate.

When Valerie Alexander came into the drawing-room just before the dinner guests were expected to arrive, she found her son alone in the room, standing with a glass of whisky in his hand at the window that overlooked the harbour. She frowned worriedly when she saw that he hadn't changed yet for dinner but was still wearing his denims and a striped cotton pullover sweater. Or was he again not going to join them? Indeed in the three days since he'd arrived, he'd hardly eaten any meals at all.

He must have heard the rustle of her long taffeta skirt because he turned abruptly, shaken out of his thoughts.

Quickly, she assumed a tranquil expression. He hated it if she worried or fussed over him, but it was difficult for her to help herself when he showed up unexpectedly and unannounced, and in so dark a mood. Clearly something had happened that upset him. She doubted if it were a woman. Over the last couple of years she'd given up hoping he'd get involved—enough to get upset, that is— with a woman. So it must be something to do with his work. Jon was too sensitive, too quick to take offence, and far too unforgiving, and he had been since he was a child. She loved him dearly, but had never been blind to his faults. Still, few mothers had such an accomplished son to be proud of.

'Won't you be joining us tonight?' she pressed gently. 'Hilda's preparing leg of lamb with all the trimmings. And you've always liked the Hamiltons.'

'No thanks, Mother, not tonight.' He tossed back the rest of his drink and set the glass down on the Queen Anne side table. 'I thought I'd take the boat out.'

'But there's a gale brewing,' Valerie said, this time unable to bite back her concern.

'Not much of one.' Jon dropped a light, absent-minded kiss on her cheek. 'Don't expect me until you see me. I'll probably stay out for a couple of days.'

It was a week later—a week of aimless sailing up and down the coast, mooring for the night wherever the winds and currents had put him when the sun went down—that Jon decided his present course ... or lack thereof ... was ridiculous. Especially since this impulsive change of scene hadn't solved a thing. Only by throwing himself back into his work, he finally decided, would he be able to block out the image of those cornflower-blue eyes that haunted his days and left him tossing at night.

It was time to snap out of it, he resolved, setting a course for Sag Harbor, and to get on with his life. And the first thing he'd better do was to pick up his mail and see if Holly was creating the same havoc with his experiments as she had with his heart. Even if she was competently holding the fort, though, he was determined to release her from the last remaining week or two of her internship so that he could return to a peaceful, empty laboratory.

The report was buried in the stack of mail lying on the desk in his sitting-room. He fished it out, tore open the manila envelope, and rapidly flipped through the closely typed pages. Acute and unanticipated disappointment flooded through him when he saw that she hadn't attached a personal note—not a word—and the feeling, utterly unexpected, stunned him. He hadn't even realised he'd been hoping for something—some appeal?—from her. Good Lord, he'd got it bad. He poured himself a stiff whisky to sip while reading those impersonal, coldly objective five pages. But he never touched it, and by the time he'd finished reading he'd forgotten all about it.

For several moments he sat motionless, seeing his own actions and their resultant reactions more clearly and with less bias than he ever had before. His eyes dropped to the last page again; carefully, he re-read Holly's description of her experiment. Then he said slowly, in a tone of pure admiration, 'Well, I'll be damned . . .'

Once Holly had mailed the report off, she submerged herself in work again, and the days flew past. Sue had returned from maternity leave, Lillian was back in the botany lab ready to take over her customary reins, and suddenly it was Holly's last day at work. And not once had she received a telephone call or letter from Jon . . . not even an acknowledgement of the two reports she'd sent him over the three-week period. But then, had she really expected any?

'Remember, you can phone me any time there's a problem you think I could help with,' Holly said to Lillian. 'I included a note to Jon with my last report, reminding him that I'm starting post-graduate work in Seattle on Monday, so I'm sure he'll return soon.'

Just as soon as he was sure she was gone, she wagered forlornly with herself, and she wouldn't even have a chance to try to explain again . . . or to apologise . . . or just to say goodbye. More than that she hadn't even fantasised. Jon wasn't the kind of man to renew an offer humbly once he'd been turned down.

'I hope so,' Lillian said, cutting into Holly's thoughts. 'Listen, Holly, now that you've briefed me, why don't you take the afternoon off and rest before the seafood feed tonight? You've earned it.'

Never had Holly felt less like a party, but Anne and Paul had insisted on one as a farewell. They were worried about her, she knew, and intent on bullying her out of the apathetic depression she'd fallen into after Jon's departure. Apathetic was right; she didn't have the energy to argue with them about it.

Holly nodded her head slowly. 'I think I'll do that,' she said. 'I ... I'm a bit tired, and I have some last-minute packing to do.'

As she walked slowly out into a radiant, warm August day, she was filled with conflicting emotions: relief at being free to pick up the pieces of her life, sadness at leaving the Institute and its work, and above everything else an overwhelming melancholy. Without admitting it to herself she'd been hoping against hope that she would hear from him. And now even that hope was dead.

The sight of a familiar estate car parked in front of Dr Kirkland's house mercifully lifted her spirits. With a shout of pleasure she flew through the house's open front door and into her brother's arms.

'I had no idea you were coming,' she cried, hugging him tightly.

'We wouldn't miss the party,' he grinned. 'Anne told us not to tell you. She wanted you to be surprised.'

As Holly stepped back from him to greet Mary and the baby, her brother got his first good look at her face. He halted her with a hand on her shoulder.

'What's the matter?' he said sharply, noting her bleary-eyed look, her pale complexion, the lines of exhaustion on her young face. 'Have you been sick? Why didn't you tell us?'

'I haven't, really . . . It's nothing. I've just been working too hard, I guess.'

Clint's hand tightened. Holly recognised all the familiar signs of his flashing temper. 'How could that damned Alexander——?'

'Jon's been out of town practically since I got back from Quinault,' she interrupted quickly, 'so you can't blame him.'

Mary's eyebrows rose, but she sensed Holly's distress and laid a restraining hand on her husband's arm. 'It looks like what Holly needs now is a nap, not an argument,' she interjected, 'if she's going to enjoy her party.'

Flashing her sister-in-law a grateful smile, Holly took Clint Junior from her. 'I'll have one as soon as I greet this little fellow.' She laughed with delight as the infant clutched her finger with his tiny, stubby fist. 'It's only been a few weeks and how he's grown!'

'He should have. He eats like a horse,' Clint said wryly, but happy pride was written all over his face.

'And why not,' Mary said, taking the baby and handing him to Clint, 'since he takes after you!' She propelled Holly towards the stairs. 'Now don't come down before six. I'll call you.'

Holly went reluctantly, but to her surprise she fell fast asleep the moment she lay down, and when Mary roused her just after six, she felt rested and relaxed.

'Hop to it,' Mary said. 'There's already a crowd down at the beach,' She set a white box on the foot of the twin bed.

'What's that?' Holly asked, yawning and pushing her tousled, dark hair out of her eyes.

'A little something from Clint and me—for you to wear tonight. We wanted to thank you for dropping everything to help out when the baby came.'

'Are you serious?' Holly said affectionately. 'After what you two have done for me——' She stopped abruptly, gasping as she parted the tissue paper wrapping to find a beautiful and extremely sexy bright red bathing-suit, and a matching wrapover skirt. She held up the scanty, sleek swimsuit. 'Clint helped pick *this* out?'

'Are you kidding?' Mary laughed. 'If he'd had his way in the shop, he'd have brought you a neck-to-toe sack from the hardware department! Now, go and take a shower and get dressed. I'm starving, and we can't eat without you, can we?'

Maybe when you're made to act happy, Holly reflected when the party was in full swing, you automatically started to feel a little better. The smile she'd plastered on her face to avoid a third-degree interrogation from her brother had begun to feel almost natural by the time she'd taken a swim and feasted on pit-steamed clams, cracked Dungeness crab, and salmon that had been baked Indian-style around a beach fire.

Still, she did find the crowd of people, the unending chatter of conversation, and the happy laughter a bit of a strain, and was relieved when Mary accepted her offer to put the baby to bed.

'As soon as everyone's eaten,' Mary said, relinquishing the sleepy, fretful baby, 'we'll come and join you. We'll move the whole party up to the house for dessert and coffee.'

'Don't hurry on my account,' Holly said. 'I haven't had a chance to hold him all evening. Lillian and Anne have been hogging him.'

'Anne, especially,' agreed Mary. In a conspiratorial whisper she added, 'Did you notice how pale around the gills Paul gets every time he sees her with the baby? And yet he can't stay away from her.' She giggled, something she didn't do very often. 'I think his bachelor days are about over.'

'I hope you're right,' Holly sighed. 'They'd be perfect for each other.' And at least some good would have come out of this ghastly summer. She took the baby into her arms and slowly walked up to the house, crooning him to sleep before she got there.

Clint Junior woke only while she sponge-bathed him, and by the time she'd put his nappy on and pulled a cotton nightgown over his head he was contentedly sucking his little fist and drifting off again.

'Why I should find you so sweet,' Holly murmured to him while she tucked him into his portable bed, 'I'll never know. Do you know, I've come to the conclusion that you're responsible for my broken heart?'

'And is it still broken?' The gruff, masculine voice came from the doorway.

Holly turned, the blood draining from her face.

'I guess it is,' he said slowly, while she stared

speechlessly at him. 'You look as if you haven't slept for a week.'

Her chin went up and the colour rose back into her cheeks. If he'd come back to gloat because she'd been suffering—which he obviously hadn't been doing: with that golden tan he looked healthier and more attractive than ever—she wasn't going to let him get away with it.

Clenching her hands she drew in a ragged breath. 'I wasn't aware that I didn't look well. I got quite a few compliments tonight.'

It wasn't a lie, either. With her soft colouring and her hair cascading in a dark cloud down her back, she was stunning. The vivid bathing-suit hugged every curve, and the flared, ruffled skirt was deceptively demure at first glance, but whenever she moved, a side slit opened to reveal a tantalising glimpse of long, shapely leg. It had caught every male eye more than once, and now it caught Jon's. His glance had dropped to it, almost automatically, when she whirled around, but then he slowly raised his eyes, studying her.

'The first time I saw you I knew you'd be beautiful in red.' If it was a compliment you'd never know it from his eyes, as fierce and penetrating as she'd ever seen them. 'But I still say you look run down.'

She met his eyes bravely. 'All right,' she admitted, 'I might have missed a little sleep for a night or two, but I'm fine now, thank you.'

'Liar,' he muttered softly. He walked past her to the portable cot and stared down at the sleeping infant for what seemed like a long time.

'You said he was responsible. Did he make you want to give up your career and become a mother yourself? Was that it?'

'No,' she said. 'Not the way you put it.' With a quiet conviction dredged up from somewhere, she tried to explain. 'Going home for a week and being there when the baby came just reminded me that some kind of family life is terribly important to me—as important as my career. Whether it includes having children or not I don't know yet. But I know I want the option ...' Her voice trailed off, stopped by a sudden swell of emotion. 'I hadn't thought it all out when I came back here—I hadn't thought it out at all—and when you asked me to marry you so ... so surprisingly, I ... I guess I hesitated.' She turned away from him to hide the tears that wouldn't stay down. 'I hurt you, and I'm sorry.'

'You hurt me all right,' he said bluntly. Holly felt his hands on her arms and found herself turned towards him, looking at him through a blur of tears. 'It was like a punch in the face, one I never saw coming.'

'Jon, I didn't mean to——'

'A punch I needed to wake me up,' he interrupted. 'I didn't realise it at the time, but you were right. I was going about things all wrong.'

'What——'

Jon stopped her again, but with a kiss that time. He crushed her so tightly she could scarcely breathe. As his lips travelled from her mouth to her eyelids, and then to her throat, he murmured, 'I promise you equal time, darling, for anything

you want. We'll have *ten* kids if you want them.'
Then his lips claimed hers again, this time with a
fierce possessiveness that took her breath away
entirely.

When at last he pulled back a few inches so that
they could breathe again, Holly whispered, 'Oh,
Jon, I love you so ... I've been so miserable ...
Don't ever leave me again. Promise!'

'Only if you marry me,' he said teasingly. But
the tone was a façade, Holly knew, because she
caught the underlying edge of anxiety in his
voice—and vulnerability too. How much he must
love her to swallow his pride and ask her a second
time!

'Immediately.' She gave him a weak grin.
'Having ten kids out of wedlock doesn't appeal to
me at all.'

The look of love and tenderness that filled his
eyes swelled Holly's heart so much she thought she
might expire on the spot. He opened his mouth to
speak, closed it, paused, then drawled. 'Ten? I
thought I said two.'

'Ten,' she replied, now grinning broadly, 'but I
won't hold you to it.' She burrowed more deeply
against his chest, ready to burst with happiness.
'We have to have some time for your research.'

'Not to mention *your* research,' he said wryly,
'and your postgraduate studies too.' He leaned his
cheek against her head, kissed her hair, and tilted
her chin up to look seriously at her. 'You know,
when I read your report and saw what you were
doing with your experiment, it made me face up to
some hard facts.'

A look she had never seen in his face before had crept into his eyes. If she hadn't known him better she might have said it was sheepishness. 'I had to admit I was wrong,' he continued. 'I'd lost a lot in the past by not having budding researchers like you around—not to mention colleagues. You were right; I was being selfish and bull-headed by refusing to work alongside other botanists—academics or not.'

She wrinkled her brow. 'But how did my little experiment do that? It was just a small variation . . . a slight twist on an old idea.'

'But a good one! I guess I was too close to my work to think of it.'

'But why didn't you call me when you got the report? It was almost two weeks ago. In fact,' she said, pique rising, 'why didn't you come back, instead of lying around in the sun while I was pining away?'

'Oh, I wasn't lying around in the sun, I was sailing——'

'Same difference——'

He ignored her words, as usual. '——to pass the time while waiting for the negotiations to be completed.' He pulled away from her so he could reach a thick, white envelope in his inside pocket.

'Negotiations?'

He handed her the envelope. 'The Alexander Institute, including its ex-director—who is now only chief of research, thank God—was snapped up, rather greedily, I must say, by one of the biggest ivy-league universities in the country. A caravan of administrator-types will be descending any minute.' He shook his head ruefully, 'Can you imagine, they've already got their architect drawing up plans for expansion.' He grinned. 'Well, I guess all those botanical researchers and postgraduate students they're planning to send will need some place to work. And you were so right about me having more time for my research . . . and my own life.'

Holly was so happy she couldn't think of anything to say.

'And since you're marrying me,' he continued, 'I don't have to worry about any predatory young undergraduates . . .'

She laughed with delight and he joined her. Then, as if he'd had enough of talking, he locked his arms around her again and kissed her hungrily. She returned it as passionately, her hands travelling through his hair and over his broad back, clasping him tightly to her.

A startling, ear-splitting wail made them jump apart.

'Damn,' Jon muttered exasperatedly, sternly eyeing his nephew-to-be, who stopped crying the instant his aunt picked him up, 'I bet your brother has him trained to do that if he sees you kissing anyone.'

Holly laughed. 'Don't be silly, he's only four weeks old.'

'Four weeks or not, I know a possessive, protective, aggressive male when I see one,' Jon retorted in a mock growl as he reached out and gently tickled the baby under his tiny chin. 'Look at that jawline,' he added, beaming when Clint

Junior responded to the friendly overtures of his uncle-to-be with a gurgle.

'Yes, I never noticed how much it looks like yours,' she rejoined drily. Then, impishly, she added, 'If Clint's got him trained, then we'd better get married right away all right.'

Jon, looking inordinately pleased with himself, drew another envelope from his pocket. 'Tickets for a flight to Reno tomorrow, then off to the South of France for a honeymoon and a well-deserved vacation for you . . . for me too.'

'You mean you bought areoplane tickets without asking me?' As lovable as he was when he was vulnerable, she loved him just as much when he was his usual, not-to-be-denied, overconfident self. 'You just assumed——'

'You'd better believe it.' His green eyes twinkled. 'Of course, I can always take them back . . .'

'Don't you dare,' Holly said, returning her nephew to his cot and coming happily back into Jon's arms. 'The only tickets I'd like better would be ones for tonight.'

He kissed her firmly on the lips. 'Never mind the tickets. Who says I'm not throwing you over my shoulder and dragging you off to my den tonight? I've got plans for you, young woman.'

'Plans?'

'Yes, plans. For one thing, I think those damned dishes are still in the dishwasher, and somebody's got to sort out how to start it. And after that I'll think of something else, believe you me.' With a sudden swoop he dipped down and swung her up into his arms.

She choked with happy laugher. 'But——'

'No buts,' he said his voice lowering huskily. 'I've a good hundred and ninety pounds and sixty inches on Junior, and as for your brother—when I wasn't sailing, I was practising my boxing.'

'Holly couldn't stop giggling. 'Are you serious?'

He took two steps towards the door, then stopped and put her down. 'Well, I guess I can wait until tomorrow for the sake of family unity,' he groaned, his eyes taking in her face with incredible, glowing tenderness. 'But we'd better go and find some company. I don't trust myself alone with you.'

She looked up at him provocatively through her long, black lashes, 'And tomorrow . . .?'

'Stop that, vixen,' he said, laughing. He removed her arms from around his neck, pulled her by the hand towards the sounds of people spilling into the downstairs rooms. But just before they started to descend the stairs, he drew her close for one exquisitely gentle kiss, then murmured into her ear,

'And tomorrow you won't be getting off so easily.'

Six exciting series for you every month... from Harlequin

Harlequin Romance·
The series that started it all

Tender, captivating and heartwarming...
love stories that sweep you off to faraway places
and delight you with the magic of love.

◆

Harlequin Presents·
Powerful contemporary love stories...as individual as the women who read them

The No. 1 romance series...
exciting love stories for you, the woman of today...
a rare blend of passion and dramatic realism.

◆

Harlequin Superromance®
It's more than romance... it's Harlequin Superromance

A sophisticated, contemporary romance-fiction
series, providing you with a longer,
more involving read...a richer mix of complex plots,
realism and adventure.